TO ENTICE THEM

DI SAM COBBS
BOOK SEVEN

M A COMLEY

ACKNOWLEDGMENTS

Special thanks as always go to @studioenp for their superb cover design expertise.

My heartfelt thanks go to my wonderful editor Emmy, and my proofreaders Joseph and Barbara for spotting all the lingering nits.

Thank you also to my amazing ARC Group who help to keep me sane during this process.

To Mary, gone, but never forgotten. I hope you found the peace you were searching for my dear friend. I miss you each and every day.

ALSO BY M A COMLEY

Blind Justice (Novella)

Cruel Justice (Book #1)

Mortal Justice (Novella)

Impeding Justice (Book #2)

Final Justice (Book #3)

Foul Justice (Book #4)

Guaranteed Justice (Book #5)

Ultimate Justice (Book #6)

Virtual Justice (Book #7)

Hostile Justice (Book #8)

Tortured Justice (Book #9)

Rough Justice (Book #10)

Dubious Justice (Book #11)

Calculated Justice (Book #12)

Twisted Justice (Book #13)

Justice at Christmas (Short Story)

Prime Justice (Book #14)

Heroic Justice (Book #15)

Shameful Justice (Book #16)

Immoral Justice (Book #17)

Toxic Justice (Book #18)

Overdue Justice (Book #19)

Unfair Justice (a 10,000 word short story)

Irrational Justice (a 10,000 word short story)

Seeking Justice (a 15,000 word novella)
Caring For Justice (a 24,000 word novella)
Savage Justice (a 17,000 word novella)
Justice at Christmas #2 (a 15,000 word novella)
Gone in Seconds (Justice Again series #1)
Ultimate Dilemma (Justice Again series #2)
Shot of Silence (Justice Again series #3)
Taste of Fury (Justice Again series #4)
Crying Shame (Justice Again series #5)
To Die For (DI Sam Cobbs #1)
To Silence Them (DI Sam Cobbs #2)
To Make Them Pay (DI Sam Cobbs #3)
To Prove Fatal (DI Sam Cobbs #4)
To Condemn Them (DI Sam Cobbs #5)
To Punish Them (DI Sam Cobbs #6)
To Entice Them (DI Sam Cobbs #7)
Forever Watching You (DI Miranda Carr thriller)
Wrong Place (DI Sally Parker thriller #1)
No Hiding Place (DI Sally Parker thriller #2)
Cold Case (DI Sally Parker thriller#3)
Deadly Encounter (DI Sally Parker thriller #4)
Lost Innocence (DI Sally Parker thriller #5)
Goodbye My Precious Child (DI Sally Parker #6)
The Missing Wife (DI Sally Parker #7)
Truth or Dare (DI Sally Parker #8)
Web of Deceit (DI Sally Parker Novella with Tara Lyons)
The Missing Children (DI Kayli Bright #1)
Killer On The Run (DI Kayli Bright #2)

Hidden Agenda (DI Kayli Bright #3)

Murderous Betrayal (Kayli Bright #4)

Dying Breath (Kayli Bright #5)

Taken (DI Kayli Bright #6)

The Hostage Takers (DI Kayli Bright Novella)

No Right to Kill (DI Sara Ramsey #1)

Killer Blow (DI Sara Ramsey #2)

The Dead Can't Speak (DI Sara Ramsey #3)

Deluded (DI Sara Ramsey #4)

The Murder Pact (DI Sara Ramsey #5)

Twisted Revenge (DI Sara Ramsey #6)

The Lies She Told (DI Sara Ramsey #7)

For The Love Of... (DI Sara Ramsey #8)

Run for Your Life (DI Sara Ramsey #9)

Cold Mercy (DI Sara Ramsey #10)

Sign of Evil (DI Sara Ramsey #11)

Indefensible (DI Sara Ramsey #12)

Locked Away (DI Sara Ramsey #13)

I Can See You (DI Sara Ramsey #14)

The Kill List (DI Sara Ramsey #15)

Crossing The Line (DI Sara Ramsey #16)

Time to Kill (DI Sara Ramsey #17)

Deadly Passion (DI Sara Ramsey #18)

I Know The Truth (A Psychological thriller)

She's Gone (A psychological thriller)

Shattered Lives (A psychological thriller)

Evil In Disguise – a novel based on True events

Deadly Act (Hero series novella)

Torn Apart (Hero series #1)

End Result (Hero series #2)

In Plain Sight (Hero Series #3)

Double Jeopardy (Hero Series #4)

Criminal Actions (Hero Series #5)

Regrets Mean Nothing (Hero series #6)

Prowlers (Di Hero Series #7)

Sole Intention (Intention series #1)

Grave Intention (Intention series #2)

Devious Intention (Intention #3)

Cozy mysteries

Murder at the Wedding

Murder at the Hotel

Murder by the Sea

Death on the Coast

Death By Association

Merry Widow (A Lorne Simpkins short story)

It's A Dog's Life (A Lorne Simpkins short story)

A Time To Heal (A Sweet Romance)

A Time For Change (A Sweet Romance)

High Spirits

The Temptation series (Romantic Suspense/New Adult Novellas)

Past Temptation

Lost Temptation

Clever Deception (co-written by Linda S Prather)

Tragic Deception (co-written by Linda S Prather)

Sinful Deception (co-written by Linda S Prather)

CHAPTER 1

"I'm so excited about this week. We've been intending to visit this area for years, and now, I can't believe we're here." Tara squeezed her husband's hand and smiled at him from the passenger seat of their smart new Lexus. The past few months had been a whirlwind for them both.

A promotion for Daniel, one that he had richly deserved. He was now a manager at the insurance firm he had worked at for five years or more. He loved his job, although his workload had increased significantly with the new role, the only downside from what Tara could tell so far. She had groaned the second she'd seen him slotting a few files into the pocket of the suitcase, for him to 'look over' in the evening once they got back from a walk on the fells.

She couldn't fall out with him, though, he was keen on his job and eager to make a good impression. He had always been a determined individual, and she couldn't see that changing anytime soon. They had been together for almost ten years, married for the last six months. Each day was like a new adventure to Tara. No man had treated her as well as he had; he worshipped her. Valued her opinion on everything, from what to have for breakfast to how he should spend his money.

This week away, in the secluded cottage they had stumbled across online, was the honeymoon they had failed to fit in at the time of the wedding. The past couple of years had seen everyone in the world make personal sacrifices due to the pandemic. Now that was over, or near enough, they had booked the cottage on a whim and, judging by their spectacular surroundings, Tara knew they wouldn't be disappointed with their decision.

"Are we there yet?" she asked, her voice childlike with high-pitched excitement.

Daniel grinned. "As it happens, yes, we are." He indicated and pulled into the dirt track. "Damn, the car is going to take a battering driving in and out of this place all week."

"Maybe we should have brought my wreck instead."

"It'll be all right, if we take it nice and steady. I hope it's not too far, but I'm inclined to think the opposite is true." He pointed ahead at the expanse of open views and lack of houses in their proximity.

"Just take your time, we're in no rush. Hard to believe that roads like this still exist these days. You wouldn't find one this bad in our neck of the woods."

He laughed. "Are you certain about that? I'm sure you would in some of the smaller villages around Coventry. Never mind, we're not going to let it spoil our holiday, are we?"

"We'll do our best."

The car rounded the next bend, and there, standing proud like something out of a scene from a romantic movie, stood a quaint thatched cottage, all on its own, surrounded by fields and the stunning views of the mountains in the near distance.

"Oh my." Tara expelled a breath and found it difficult to suppress the emotions surging within.

"Hey, are you all right, Mrs Mansell?"

She turned to smile at him, her eyes watering. "Never better. This place is amazing. Being here, alone with you, is going to be utterly mind-blowing this week."

"It sure is. The boy did good choosing this place then, eh?"

"Undoubtedly. I love it—not as much as I love you, though."

He lifted her hand to his mouth and kissed the back of it. "You're worth every penny and more. This week is going to be one to remember, I guarantee it."

"Sounds perfect to me."

"Oh, hang on a second, looks like we've got company."

Tara twisted in her seat and peered over her shoulder. "Are we expecting anyone to join us?"

"No. Ah, I know who it is, it's probably the woman from the agency. When I asked about picking up the key, she said there was no need as she would be here to greet us."

"Phew, I was getting worried then."

"You're daft. There's never anything to fear, not while I'm around." He gave her a toothy grin.

She chuckled and reached over to kiss his cheek. "My hero. What would I do without you?"

"Hmm... let me think about that for a moment or two."

Tara smiled and settled back into her seat again to contemplate, not for the first time, how lucky she was to have Daniel as her husband.

The closer they got to the cottage, the more her heart skipped a beat. By the time Daniel drew up outside the wrought-iron gate, her pulse rate had escalated to a near dangerous level. She placed a hand between her breasts. "Be still my beating heart," she said breathlessly.

"It truly is fantastic. Hold on to that enthusiasm until our visitor leaves." He leaned in to give her a kiss.

"We're here, I'm thrilled. Thank you for making yet another dream come true, Daniel."

"It's always a pleasure doing something extra-special for you."

They hopped out of the car, and the young blonde woman did the same. She joined them at the gate and beamed.

"Welcome to Fell View Cottage. I'm Annie. I hope you've had a pleasant trip."

"It was touch and go with the traffic on the M6, as usual, but once we got past the roadworks section it was a breeze to get here. However, I do have one complaint."

Annie frowned and tilted her head. "You do? What's that? I'll see if I can correct it."

Daniel pointed behind the two cars. "You could have mentioned the dirt track when I made the initial booking, and the number of times I've spoken to you since."

"Ouch, sorry. My boss always insists on me telling the truth where our properties are concerned, it's just that I personally love this place so much, I tend to forget the one drawback it has to its name."

Daniel flicked his hand. "I'm willing to forgive you, this time. The setting is absolutely remarkable, worth taking two years off the life expectancy of my car. Well, I say that now, but I'm sure I'll be cursing you by the time I've driven up and down the road twenty times or more during the week."

They all laughed.

"You've got my number if you want to scream and shout at me at the end of the week. I'm betting that come Friday, when it's time for you to pack up and leave, you'll be ringing me to tell me there's a tip winging its way to me in the post, or is that wishful thinking on my part?"

"The price I've paid to have the privilege of staying here, I think that's highly unlikely."

"Let me show you around inside, and then I'll leave you to it so you can enjoy the peace and tranquillity this wonderful home has to offer. This truly is one of the best properties we have on offer in the area. It's fully booked throughout the holiday season."

"Just not at this time of year, not with the road being in such bad shape. Maybe have a word with the owner. Perhaps he can set some funds aside and get the road knocked into shape. Wouldn't that increase his revenue in the long run?" Daniel asked.

"You're right. Unfortunately, we get a lot of stiff comments about the road in the feedback forms, but hey-ho. You know what men can be like, though. Stubbornness is always a major trait to overcome in our line of business. Anyway, I hope you can set that aside and appreciate all the positives this place has to offer."

Tara slipped her arm through Daniel's. "I'm sure we'll have a wonderful stay. I can't wait to see what treasures await us inside."

"Then let's get in there." Annie led the way through the pretty front garden with its immaculately presented borders and opened the door to the cottage. "Come into your new abode for the week. It's all been recently renovated by the owner, you can tell he's put his heart and soul into these four walls."

The hallway was small but perfectly formed. The stairs had been stripped back to the original wood, and a new, bold, striped runner covered the treads. The banisters were made of stained wood, and the railing had been painted white.

"It's stunning. He did a good job," Tara said. She admired

the pictures on three of the walls. They appeared to be of the local area.

"If you're impressed by the hallway, the kitchen is going to blow you away."

They entered the door on the right and, again, Tara was left feeling breathless.

"It's amazing. Hard to imagine someone going to this expense when all they're going to do is rent their home out."

"I said the same to Mr Wilson myself, once he unveiled it to us last year. I actually offered to buy the cottage off him, but he refused to sell. He used the money he inherited after his mother's death to help with the renovation costs."

"Does he ever come here himself?"

"No, we rent it out all year round, or should I say it's on our books and available twelve months of the year."

"Hard to believe. I think it's a magical place, inside and out," Tara gushed. She ran her hand across the black granite worktop close to the door.

"My sentiments exactly. I'll give you the guided tour and then get out of your hair to allow you to enjoy the facilities. You don't want me hanging around, spoiling your enjoyment. There's a key to the back door hanging up on the hook there. If you can divide the rubbish up into the different coloured recycling bags as you go along, that would be wonderful. The truck comes every Thursday. Just leave it outside the cottage at the front, if you will?"

"That's fine by us." Tara nodded. "We recycle everything at home, so no big deal to continue to do the same here."

Annie smiled. "Let me show you the lounge."

She squeezed by them and turned left into a large lounge with a bay window at the front. It had a chintz padded window seat, and Tara could imagine herself sitting there, feet up, reading one of her books and glancing up now and again to take in the spectacular views.

"Exceptional. I love this place even more, and we haven't even seen upstairs yet."

"Let me remedy that now. The remote for the TV is on the table. You have Sky on hand, should you need it."

"We're not really keen on watching TV all the time. There are far more interesting things to do with our time, aren't there, love?" Daniel said with a certain glint in his eye.

Tara's cheeks warmed under his intense gaze. "Yes, sweetheart."

Annie didn't comment. She swept past them and made her way upstairs.

"You've embarrassed her now." Tara giggled.

"Tough," Daniel said and pulled her by the hand up the stairs.

"There are three bedrooms, not huge, especially the third bedroom which is more like a box room really."

"We're only interested in seeing the main bedroom," Daniel muttered.

Tara dug him in the ribs, warning him to behave. He shrugged and widened his eyes, a picture of innocence. She quashed the smile threatening to emerge.

"You're incorrigible," she whispered and shoved him ahead of her.

"As if," he said.

They followed Annie into the master bedroom and were again blown away by the fantastic scenery all around them.

"I'm lost for words," Tara whispered.

Daniel wet his finger and struck the air. "That's got to be a first. I think I've managed to achieve the unachievable."

Tara slapped his arm. "You cheeky sod. Please do excuse my impertinent husband, he tends to let his guard down whilst on holiday."

Daniel laughed and shook his head. "Tell me a man who doesn't."

Annie smiled. "I'm glad you like it here. I'm sure you're going to have a fabulous week here in The Lakes. Have you ventured up this way before?"

"No, never. It's been on our to-do list for years, but we've never got around to booking anywhere," Tara explained.

Daniel raised an eyebrow. "And why was that, love?"

Tara chewed her lip and frowned. "I can't think. Tell me."

"Because you always wanted to jet off abroad. Ignoring the fact that we have idyllic places like this to explore in this country."

Tara held her hands up. "Guilty as charged. After the scorcher of a summer we've had this year, there really is no need to travel abroad any more."

Daniel clapped. "Hooray, it has finally sunk in."

"Although we love having visitors up here during the summer, it can be a touch annoying to the locals," Annie revealed.

"I can imagine," Tara said.

"It's the litter that really gets to me. You should see what the volunteers bring down from the top of the mountains. If hill walkers can be bothered to drag their supplies up there with them, surely, they can stuff a few empty packets in their bags to bring back down again. Oh dear, I'm sorry, my boss is always telling me to keep my opinions to myself."

"Your secret is safe with us. I can appreciate how upsetting that must be for the locals. People should have more respect for places as picturesque as this. They come here to take in the beautiful scenery and end up leaving it littered. It's selfish and there's no reason on earth why that should happen."

"Thank you. I wish everyone was as understanding as you are. Sadly, you're in a minority. Anyway, that's the tour completed, except to tell you that the bathroom is next door. You don't tend to get en suites in older properties. The owner fought hard to cling on to a certain amount of charm, hence the reason he refused to turn the box room into an en suite. I think he was wrong, but again, that's just my opinion."

"I'm in two minds about making changes like that, so I can see both sides of the argument," Tara said.

Annie held the door to the bathroom open. Tara poked her head around the door and took in the large grey tiles and stylish chrome accessories.

"Yet another superb addition."

Annie smiled. "Glad you like it. Okay, I'm going to leave you now. I'll let myself out. You've got my number. Give me a call if you need any further assistance while you're here."

"You're too kind. Do you live locally?" Tara asked.

The three of them went back downstairs and stopped at the front door.

"Not far up the road, about fifteen minutes away. Have a wonderful stay."

"We will. Thanks again, Annie. Enjoy the rest of your evening."

"Oh, I will. Life is what you make it, after all."

"Exactly." Tara waved her off and then closed the door.

Daniel had his arms open. She walked into them and smiled up at him.

"Thank you for choosing the perfect place for our honeymoon."

"I'm delighted with the way it has turned out." He bent to kiss her and then pulled back. "I'm going to get the bags in. I'd love a cup of coffee. There should be a welcome pack in the kitchen. I hope there is, I paid extra for one."

"Strange that Annie didn't mention it. I'll have a look in the cupboards, see what I can find."

Daniel left the cottage, and Tara ventured into the kitchen. She opened the fridge and found a carton of semi-skimmed milk, then searched the cupboard on the left and discovered tea bags, a jar of coffee and a small bag of sugar. She filled the kettle and then went out to the car to help Daniel with their belongings.

"Any luck?" he asked. "I hope so. I don't fancy going back out just yet."

"Yep, we struck gold. All the basics we need, for now. We can go to the supermarket tomorrow."

"Maybe they'll deliver." Daniel laughed.

"We'll see. We might need a breather from this place in the morning."

"Can you grab the two overnight bags for me?"

Tara picked up the bags Daniel had put on the road behind the car and took them into the cottage. He followed her in with the suitcase and his sports holdall.

"I told you not to pack too much. This lot weighs a ton."

"I had to bring the essentials, didn't I?" Tara beamed at him and led the way up the stairs.

"I'll leave you to unpack and I'll make the drink. Coffee?"

"Sounds great to me. Well, the second half. Not sure if I can cope with unpacking all the bags myself."

"Typical. I'll be back in a tick."

Tara noted the time on the bedside clock; it was just after five-thirty. Her stomach rumbled. Daniel rejoined her, and together they made light work of the unpacking and then collapsed on the bed half an hour later.

"What are we going to do about dinner?"

He dropped a hand down beside the bed and held up a pizza. "I shoved this in while your back was turned."

"Aww… you really do think of everything, don't you?"

He pulled her in for a kiss. "Most of the time, yes. Now then, as this is supposed to be our honeymoon, I think an early night is in order, don't you?"

"Are you kidding me? Maybe after we've eaten, definitely

not before. I'll go and put it in the oven now. It'll only take twenty minutes." She wriggled out of his grasp before he had a chance to pin her to the bed.

"Spoilsport. Shame I never thought to drop a few beers into the bag as well."

"I'm sure we'll cope."

Tara grabbed the pizza and ran down the stairs. Thankfully, the oven was similar to the one they had at home. She put it on 180C and found a flat tray inside on which she placed the pizza.

Daniel came down ten minutes later, wearing his comfy joggers and a T-shirt. He slipped his arms around her waist and held her tightly. "Roll on dessert time."

She grinned up at him. "A one-track mind, like all men."

"I won't argue, and I don't hear you complaining, ever."

"Okay, you've got me on that one. Sit at the table. Actually, you can find the cutlery for me and lay it."

"How long is it going to be?"

"About eight inches, the same as usual."

He groaned. "Hold on, I'm supposed to be the one with a one-track mind."

"Just giving you a run for your money. Ten minutes. I'll turn the oven up a little, see if that will hurry it along."

AFTER THEY'D DEMOLISHED their pizza, they took a glass of wine upstairs, and Daniel fulfilled his promise of supplying her with dessert. They snoozed for a little, and then Daniel got out of bed to fetch the rest of the bottle of wine they'd forgotten to take up with them. He threw on some clothes and wandered through to the kitchen where he found the back door ajar.

"Strange, I don't remember either of us going out into the garden." He closed the door and locked it, retrieved the bottle of wine from the fridge and went back into the hallway. A noise in the lounge caught his attention. He crept closer to the crack in the door. As far as he could make out, there was nothing there. Taking another few steps, he poked his head into the room. Suddenly, a whack sent him crashing to the floor.

"What the fu…?" His neck felt heavy, enough to give him trouble lifting his head. Some kind of thick stick was placed under his chin, forcing him to glance up.

A person dressed all in black and wearing a balaclava towered over him. Daniel gulped.

"Thank you for joining me." The voice sounded automated, unless his hearing had been affected by the hit he had received.

"Who are you? What are you doing in our cottage?"

"You, me and wifey upstairs are going to have a little fun."

"Fun? No, please, don't rape her. Don't do that!"

The intruder struck him around the face with the stick. "You think you're in a position to tell me what I can and can't do?"

Daniel held the side of his face, a welt surfacing under his fingers accompanied the residual stinging. "Yes, I'm sorry. Do what you want to me, but leave her out of it, I'm begging you."

"Begging doesn't wash with me either. Call her downstairs."

Daniel shook his head. "I won't do it. No, punish me, not her."

The stick rose in the air again and landed on the other side of his face. This time a thorn caught his skin, and a thin spray of blood squirted across the room. The pain caught him off-guard. "What do you want from me?"

"I've told you once. I'm not in the habit of repeating myself. Now, do it!"

"I won't. You can't make me."

The intruder took another step closer and withdrew a knife. The blade touched the tip of Daniel's nose and sliced off the end.

He screamed and then covered his mouth with his hand, stifling his complaint. "Why? What's this all about?"

"Call her!"

"I won't."

The knife changed direction, this time the blade carved through his right earlobe.

Daniel cried out and cupped it with his hand. Tears scorched his eyes, and the pizza he'd eaten earlier forced its way into his throat. "Don't do this. We're renting this place for the week. If you're after money, we never carry cash on us. We always use our cards. I can go to an ATM and get out a max of between two-fifty and three hundred, if that will help? Just please, don't hurt us. We're newly married and we have our whole lives ahead of us."

The knife swished back and forth barely three inches from his face. Daniel turned his head away.

"Call her down or I'll pop your eyes out, one at a time, and squish them underfoot. Do it!"

"Ta... Tara, can you come down here, love?"

The intruder leaned in and whispered, "I knew you would see sense... eventually. Don't push me again, you hear me?"

"As clear as a bell. I promise."

"What do you want, Daniel? I'm not dressed. My clothes are lying in a heap on the bedroom floor, where you left them."

"Throw something on and come down here. I need to see you. Don't keep me waiting too long now."

"I like that. You're enticing her to come to you with the promise of another sex session at the end of it. You're a very wise man when you're at breaking point, aren't you?"

"When she comes down, don't hurt her, please," Daniel pleaded for the umpteenth time.

"We'll have to see about that, won't we? It depends on how you react in the meantime."

"I'll behave. I just want us to get out of this situation safely… and alive. I wish I knew what you wanted. I would bend over backwards to give it to you, if only you would leave the house now. We're not wealthy people. We're rich in only one thing, love. I adore her…" He fell silent as the stairs creaked.

Daniel closed his eyes, shutting out the image of the knife still angled towards his face. He had to swallow down the temptation to call out and warn Tara to run, not to set foot into the lounge, but the fear of what this person was going to do to either of them made him rethink.

Please, God, don't let him do this to her, to us. Deliver us safely from this terrible experience. Give me the chance to get us out of here alive.

"Babe, where are you?" Tara called out.

"In the lounge."

"What are you doing, playing hide-and-seek? Is this another one of your sex gam—?" Tara appeared in the doorway and was struck dumb the second she laid eyes on the intruder.

"Come in, Tara, join us," the automated voice boomed.

Her gaze shifted quickly between Daniel and the person holding the pair of them captive.

"Just do as they say and don't make a fuss, love," Daniel warned, not knowing what else to say.

"Listen to him. Sit down in the chair opposite, we're going to play a little game."

In a confused daze, Tara sat. She had tugged Daniel's T-shirt down over her slender legs. "Game, what game? Daniel, are you okay? My God, your ear," she whispered in a scared babble.

The intruder laughed. "That's nothing. Wait until the real games begin."

"Why us?" Daniel asked. "I've offered you money to leave us alone. What else can I do to persuade you not to hurt us?"

"Nothing. So keep your mouth shut. Speak only when you're spoken to, got that?"

"Please, Daniel, do as you're told," Tara pleaded.

Daniel inhaled a breath and let it gush out. "If I don't put up a fight, who knows where this will all end?"

The knife whooshed closer to his face. "If you want to take the risk, don't let me stop you, wise-arse."

Tara reached out a hand. "Please, he's only trying to protect me. Don't hurt him. What can we do to make you leave? What do you need? If money isn't an option, then what will it take?"

"I want... no, I'll leave it there for now." The intruder removed a long piece of rope from their pocket and threw it at Daniel. "Tie her hands behind her back."

"And if I refuse?"

No sooner had he said the words than the blade cut a deep trail through Daniel's right cheek. He gasped as the white heat of pain shot through him.

"Daniel. Do as instructed, please, stop messing about."

Tears dripped onto his bloodstained cheeks. "I won't do it. You're going to have to kill me before I enter into any warped game you have in mind. We deserve better than this."

The blade swished dangerously from side to side and then zeroed in on its target, Daniel's other earlobe, slicing it off. Daniel's gaze followed it to the floor. He shook his head in disgust, and the rage built like a furnace inside. "I will not be treated like this. Do your worst to me, just leave Tara out of this."

"Tie her up or I'll start taking chunks out of her. The choice is yours."

Daniel angrily clawed at his face, wiping away the tears now mixed with the blood seeping from his various wounds. "I can't, no, I *won't*."

Neither he nor Tara saw it coming. The knife was swiftly swung in her direction and carved a deep line in her right cheek. She stared at Daniel, the shock registering in her eyes along with disbelief. A scream left her trembling lips.

"No. Please, no more. I'll tie her up. Babe, you're going to have to forgive me."

Tara shook her head. "Don't do this, Daniel. We'll get through this together. Don't let the bastard drive a wedge between us."

He swallowed the acid burning his throat and picked up the piece of rope draped over his bare leg. "I have to protect you. If this is the only way, then so be it, love."

Tara refused to give him her hands and kept them tucked close to her chest. Daniel had to grip her wrists tightly, forcing her to obey him.

"No, Daniel. I won't allow it."

She tried to headbutt him, but he saw it coming and dodged out of the way.

Then he was compelled to do something he never thought he'd need to do. He struck her with his fist, hard, on the jaw. Her head lolled to the side; she was out cold. He flopped back into the chair, the wind sucked out of him, and glared at the intruder. "You bastard."

"I am. Bravo! Now, wake her up again."

"I refuse to play along with your game any longer, you hear me? Do your bloody worst to me. I will not hurt my wife… not again," he corrected himself.

"I think you're forgetting who's in charge here. Still, it's your loss. Give me your hands."

Daniel held his hands up in front of him, his gaze never leaving Tara. His emotions jumbled, his nerves jangled and pulled tautly. The rope was bound firmly around his wrists. What was he supposed to do now? How could he keep them safe when he was trussed up and rendered useless? "Don't do this. Let's talk about what you need. Name it, and I'll get it for you."

"I want you to shut the fuck up." The intruder lashed out and struck Daniel around the face and then turned their attention on Tara. Two swipes, one on each cheek with a gloved hand and Tara stirred. "Nice to have you back in the room with us. Listen very carefully, Tara. If you want to save yourself, I'm going to need you to do something for me. Are you up for that?"

"Yes, I don't want to die. What do you want me to do? I'm prepared to do anything to get us out of this situation."

"Hmm… well then, I need you to kill your husband in order to save yourself."

"No! I won't… I can't do it! I'll do anything but that." Tara screamed.

Daniel's heart swelled. He'd never been prouder of Tara than he was at that moment. Still, he wouldn't allow this deplorable human being to coerce her into doing the unthinkable—or not, as the case may be. "Tara, if you have to kill me to save your own skin, then you have my permission. But remember this, I will always love you, no matter what happens next."

The intruder slow-clapped his speech. "You're to be admired, both of you. It's not solving the problem, though, is it? Tara, you're going to have to kill him, if your ultimate aim here is to be set free, to save yourself."

Tears seeped onto his wife's cheeks. Her gaze locked with his, pleading for guidance on what to do next. "Please, Daniel, help me out. I don't know what to do. We made a pact that if anything ever happened to either one of us, the other would go as well."

"That was a silly pact. If I remember rightly, we were drunk at the time. I love you, Tara, and no matter if our lives end here or not, I will never stop loving you. You're the most caring, loving person I know. Candid at times, but people know where they stand with you. Don't let this bastard alter that. Do what you need to do to survive, my love."

"There, he's given you his permission, not that you needed it in the first place because it's my instructions that matter, *not his*. This is all becoming rather tiresome now. Kill him."

"How? I mean, no, I won't… I can't, don't make me do this."

The knife slashed Tara's other cheek. She cried out and stared at Daniel. "What should I do?"

"You're going to have to do what's in your heart, Tara."

The intruder stood between them, interrupting their ability to hold eye contact. "Listen to me, Tara, *not him*. I'm going to give you the knife and I want you to slice his throat, nice and deep. It'll be over soon enough. One swipe, that's all it's going to take."

"And what happens to Tara then?" Daniel shouted.

"Then I'll set her free."

The knife was placed in Tara's hand, and the intruder stepped out of the way. "I'm going to give you ten seconds to fulfil my command."

"No, I refuse." Tara stared at the blade she was now holding.

"Then I will have no hesitation in killing both of you. The choice is yours. Five. Four. Three. Two…"

Tara got to her feet and lashed out at the intruder instead of Daniel. Daniel couldn't believe his eyes. Either Tara was braver than he thought or downright stupid, he didn't have time to figure out which.

The intruder thumped his wife in the face. The knife dropped to the floor. Undeterred, Tara flew after the blade, but the intruder had other ideas. The knife was kicked under the sofa, leaving them both empty-handed and staring at each other.

"That was foolish. Don't think that's the only weapon I brought with me—it isn't."

Tara grunted as another fist connected with her stomach.

"I won't allow you to win." Tara's hands flattened in a karate pose.

Daniel had momentarily forgotten about his wife's love of martial arts. He watched, fascinated, at the exchange now that all they had between them were their bare hands and no other weapons at their disposal. Tara had practised a few moves on him over the years, so he knew she had it in her to handle herself with assurance.

Tara and the intruder circled the room, each of them waiting for the opportunity to take the other down. The intruder was the first to lunge. Tara dodged the attack and then chopped the intruder on the back of the neck. The intruder plummeted to the floor but jumped back to their feet quickly.

"You'll pay for that." Another knife, a flick knife, appeared, and jabbed at Tara.

She shunted back with each thrust until she found herself pinned against the wall.

"This isn't how I envisaged the ending, but you forced my arm." The intruder thrust the knife into Tara's stomach and twisted it.

Tara stood there, doubled over, staring first at her attacker and then down at the knife embedded in her stomach.

"No. Tara. No!" Daniel shouted.

But it was too late. Tara dropped to her knees. Every movement after that seemed to happen in slow motion until her face hit the floor. She was dead.

Now Daniel was on his own.

"I warned you what would happen. You're to blame. You should have carried out my instructions when I told you to."

Daniel continued to stare at the prostrate figure of his wife. He rose to his feet but was knocked back down again. "Kill me, I dare you. Then all of this will have been for nothing because you won't have got anything out of this sham."

"That's what you think. I will leave here with the satisfaction of knowing that I ended two lives tonight, that's all I ever wanted."

"What? Why? Go on, tell me, what have you got to lose now? I'll be dead in five minutes, judging by the look of determination I can see in your eyes."

"Correct. You will never know. I don't have to reveal my motive to you or anyone else. Knowing that you'll both be dead in a matter of minutes is good enough for me."

"You're warped, worse than that, a depraved individual who doesn't deserve to walk this earth."

"Absolutely. I'm not about to deny it."

"Finish me off. Get it out of the way and leave us to be together once more."

"That would be too easy. No, I have bigger and better plans for you."

Daniel frowned. "Meaning?"

"Meaning, sit there while I tie your feet together." The intruder removed another length of rope from their jacket pocket and got down on one knee, their gaze locked on Daniel's, warning him to stay still while the rope was wrapped around his ankles. "There, that's a good boy. See how pleasant I can be when people listen and comply with my wishes?"

"Screw you. Get it over with. Stop revelling in this torturous situation."

"Stop telling me what to do. You're nobody to me. No one orders me around. The quicker you understand that the better."

"Shut up. I have nothing left I want to say to you." Daniel's gaze remained on his dead wife. All he wanted to do now was lie down beside her and die. He wanted to go to Heaven with her, never to be separated again.

The intruder thrust Daniel back on the sofa and then wandered over to Tara's body. Daniel watched in horror what happened next. Tara's body was set alight. Daniel screamed and struggled to break free from his bindings, but they held firm. He closed his eyes, not wanting to see Tara engulfed in the flames.

Farewell my love, until we meet again.

The intruder approached Daniel once more, knife in hand, and tilted his head back. It was all over in a second Daniel could see Tara clearly, just ahead of him.

Tara, wait for me, I'm right behind you.

CHAPTER 2

"Chris, no, don't do it… no!"

The car exploded. Sam shot up in bed and buried her head in her hands. That night, the night Chris had committed suicide, had torn her life apart. The nightmares had started and hadn't let up ever since. That was over a week ago. She was an absolute wreck. She turned to stare at the empty bed beside her. There was no indent in the pillow where Rhys's head should be. Was her life truly worth living, now that he was gone, too?

Sonny whimpered in the corner, waiting patiently for her to call him over. "Come here, boy. Mummy needs a cuddle."

Her cockapoo bolted onto the bed and took up his position, lying across her legs. Her head flopped against his, the smell of him comforting her, which even the alcohol had failed to do over the past week or so.

I had everything... and now it's all gone. I dread to think what lies around the corner. What the future holds for me, now that Rhys has gone.

Even thinking the words made her feel guilty. She'd had a

week from hell, dealing with everything that entailed laying someone she had loved in the past to rest.

She felt numb inside. Her head was filled with memories, from two separate relationships. Where once she had everything, now all she had to brighten her days was her beloved dog.

"I feel so lost and alone, Sonny," she sobbed into his fur.

He glanced over his shoulder and licked the tears flowing down her cheeks.

"I need to get on with my life. I can't keep dwelling on the past. But then, it's only been a week since I said farewell... to both of them. Why? Why did Chris have to do it, kill himself? Why didn't he just reach out to someone for the help he needed? Why? My life all but ended the night he flicked that switch on the lighter. Had that been his intention all along? To destroy my life, even when he could no longer be a part of it?"

The misery descended once more. Sam was aware of what needed to happen in order for her to continue living, but knowing it, and being prepared to do something about it, were two entirely different things. She threw back the quilt, covering Sonny in the process. He scooted out from under the covers and tilted his head as if to ask what that was all about.

"I have to get a wriggle on, boy. It's my first day back to work."

He flopped down on the bed, his head resting on his paws, his eyes following her around the room.

"Don't go giving me that look. You've had me all to yourself for the past week. Thinking about it, you'll probably be glad to see the back of me. No more doom and gloom, bringing you down. You'll love being back with Auntie Doreen, I know you will."

He let out a groan and shifted position to turn his back on

her. Sam attempted to give him a cuddle, but he was having none of it and flew off the bed and ran downstairs. Sighing, she followed him and let him out into the back garden so he could take care of his morning business. Sam filled the kettle and boiled it. She cursed loudly when she opened the fridge and found only a few dregs of milk left in the carton. That was, until she remembered she had some UHT milk at the back of one of the cupboards, stored there for emergencies.

Sonny trotted through the back door and sat next to his food bowl. She topped up his water and then offered him a handful of biscuits. Sonny sniffed the biscuits and walked away, totally disinterested in what was on offer.

"Suit yourself." She continued making her drink and then took it upstairs where she stepped into the shower. Usually, letting the hot water rain down on her satisfied her need to feel alive, but not today. Would she ever *feel alive* again, now that they were both gone?

Pack it in. Stop wallowing in self-pity. None of this is my fault. I can change what lies ahead only if I stop living in the past, dwelling on what might have been in Rhys's case. My life is a shambles. How can I recover from this?

She dressed in her navy-blue trouser suit and dried her shoulder-length hair. There, right by her ear, she noticed a stray grey one which she plucked out.

What the fuck? I'm thirty-two, for fuck's sake. That had no right presenting itself like that. Taunting me, telling me that I'm past it. I have my whole life ahead of me, haven't I? But who will I share it with? How can I trust giving my heart to someone else when it's been broken so badly?

The questions bombarded her, one after the other, until she was wrought with anguish. She had to set all her turmoil aside, for now, she couldn't turn up at work feeling this distraught and so downbeat. She just couldn't. Her life was a misery, and there was no way her boss would allow her through the main entrance if she showed her face in this state. She smiled at herself in the mirror, and her heart broke once more.

Will I ever be able to smile a genuine smile again? I doubt it. What will become of me? Will I be alone for the rest of my life? Who will want a greying, youngish woman with little to nothing to offer a man?

Sam pinched her cheeks to add some much-needed colour and then reached for her makeup bag to see if that would help make a difference to her demeanour. She doubted it, but it was definitely worth a shot. She applied the lightest of touches, not one for ever feeling the need to plaster on lashings of foundation, blusher and eyeshadow. Standing back, she was pleased with the result.

At the front door, she gathered Sonny's bag of goodies that she had topped up the night before, slipped on her shoes and coat and headed out of the door with Sonny on a leash beside her.

Doreen was standing at her front window, awaiting their arrival. She smiled and came to the front door. Worry lines had covered her temple by the time she answered it. "Hello, Sam. How are you feeling today?"

There was no fooling her wise old neighbour. "Fair to middling, I suppose. But I need to get back to work sometime."

"I know, dear. A word of caution, if I may? It has only been a week since the... um... accident. Are you sure you're up to it, after all you've been through? Tell me to butt out and stop interfering if you like, but you mean the absolute world to me and I would hate you to come home this evening regretting your decision and feeling a thousand times worse. It's been a traumatic week for you, one way or another. There, I've said my bit. It's only because I care."

Sam took a step forward and hugged Doreen. "I know

and I appreciate it. Hey, are you sure it's not because you'll be missing out on our afternoon chats?"

Doreen wrinkled her nose and laughed. "Ah, you're an excellent detective, DI Sam Cobbs, you know me so well. I've enjoyed getting to know you more this past week. There's a lot more to you than meets the eye. You're an amazing woman, and don't let any bugger tell you otherwise. Now, I repeat, are you one hundred percent sure you're ready to tackle the daily grind of being a detective inspector once more?"

"I am. I'll make you a promise. If I sense I'm being overwhelmed with my daily routine, I'll give in and come home. How's that? Believe me, I'd rather be at home with Sonny and spending the odd afternoon over a cuppa and a scone with you, my dearest friend. Unfortunately, that won't pay the bills, will it? And there are a few hefty ones looming on the horizon." She cast a glance over her shoulder at the hire car the insurance company had supplied while they sorted out her claim, since her own car had been blown up in the accident, as well as Chris's van.

"I bet you're still having nightmares about it all, aren't you?"

"One or two. I don't think that will ever alter, given that it was a life-changing incident in more ways than one." Her eyes burned with unshed tears, and she waved a hand. "Oh God, I'm off again. I'm doing my very best to stay strong, but..."

"I'm so sorry, that's the last thing I wanted to do, set you off again. Do you want me to make you a cuppa?"

"No, I'll be fine. Try not to worry about me. Once I'm at work, I'm sure I'll have plenty to occupy my mind."

"You know best, dear." Doreen smiled and held out her hand to take Sonny's lead. "If you get a chance during your busy day, would you mind giving me a quick tinkle to let me know everything is all right? You know how much I worry."

Sam hugged Doreen again. "I will, I promise. I hope Sonny won't be too disruptive for you today. I think he's got used to having me at home all day."

"He'll be fine. Just like you, I'm sure he'll slip back into his routine with Ginger soon enough."

Ginger was Doreen's cat, who Sonny adored. They were best of friends and helped to keep Doreen entertained during the day.

"Hopefully, I'll see you at around six-thirty then. Thanks again for always being there for us both, Doreen. I'd be lost without you."

"Hush now. It's always a pleasure to be of assistance. I'm going to make a beef casserole today. Fancy some when you get in?"

"Sounds delicious."

"Good. That's a load off my mind, knowing that you'll be eating a proper meal after a long day at work. I swear you've lost weight this past week."

Sam smiled and waved goodbye. "I'll see you later," she said, not willing to admit the truth. Every time she had thought about cooking a main meal, she had ended up burning it, distracted while her mind recapped the awful events of that day.

She slipped into the Ford Puma and waved a second time at Doreen who had taken up residence at the lounge window again. Sam popped on the radio and played the music louder than normal to help keep her focus on the road ahead.

Twenty minutes later, she drew up in her allocated space at the station and paused for a moment or two before she left the vehicle. Bob Jones, her partner, had pulled up not long after she had arrived and was in the process of getting out of his car.

"Hey, how's it going?"

She allowed him to forego the normal formalities when they were alone, away from the rest of the team.

"I'll let you know once I've taken a gander at what awaits me in my in-tray. How are you doing, Bob?"

"Stressed but chilled at the same time. I know, it doesn't make sense. Welcome to my world. It's good to have you back. Are you sure you're ready for this? Another week off wouldn't have made much difference, Sam."

"I feel ready. Let's just say my body is willing. We'll see what my mind has to say on the subject later. What cases are open at the moment?"

"Nothing major, thankfully. In your absence, we've managed to keep everything ticking over. We've been indebted to the local criminals for choosing to take the week off, whilst you were away." He smiled warmly.

"I bet that'll change within a few hours of me sitting at my desk."

"More than likely. Criminals and bad cases appear to get magnetically drawn to you most weeks."

They made their way towards the main entrance and, being a true gent, Bob opened the door for her.

Nick, the desk sergeant, greeted her with a cheerful smile. "Lovely to see you, ma'am. We've missed you."

"That's nice to hear, thanks, Nick."

She and Bob ascended the stairs together. The closer she got to her office, the more her intestines tightened into small knots. Her steps faltered near the top. Her actions didn't go unnoticed by Bob. He'd been wittering on beside her about the adventures he and his wife had been on over the weekend, and Sam had switched off halfway up the staircase.

Bob gently touched her arm. "Are you all right, Sam?"

"I will be, once I get today over and done with."

"If I can ease the burden on your shoulders at all, just shout."

"I'll do that. Shit, I've never experienced this kind of sensation before, not at work anyway."

"You've been through a lot. It's going to take time to get over it. I wish everything could be handled with a click of the fingers. The truth is, it can't."

"I know. I'll get there. I have a great team around me. I'm sure that's going to make all the difference come the end of the day."

"Absolutely. You know we've got your back and you can count on all of us, especially me."

Sam inhaled a steadying breath and threw open the door to the incident room. She released the breath she'd been holding in when she discovered it empty. "That's a relief. Maybe I'm not as ready as I thought I was to handle all the sympathetic glances and the words of condolences."

"It's going to take time. The team won't badger you. We're all here to support you. Just tell us if you think we're crossing the line any time."

"I will. I'd love a coffee, if you're offering."

He shuffled his feet.

She could tell something was burning his tongue. "Spit it out, Bob."

"Umm... I wanted you to know I did my best trying to deal with the post, but it kind of got on top of me the first few days and then snowballed a touch."

Sam rolled her eyes. "Thanks for the warning. Perhaps you'd better make that two cups of coffee, if there's room on my desk for them."

Bob scurried over to the drinks station, and Sam inched closer to her office. Outside the door, she paused to take in a few more breaths. The trepidation was something she had never encountered before. She hated feeling so helpless and out of control, it didn't come naturally to her.

"Are you all right?" Bob called over.

"Give me a second." She finally took the plunge and inched the door open. One look at the state her desk was in and she wished she could jack it in for the day and hurry home but, out of nowhere, her determination materialised and forced her to enter the room. She hovered at the edge of her desk and took in the view of the fells in the distance, which did their usual job of miraculously calming her jangled nerves.

Bob placed two cups of coffee on her desk and retreated. He mumbled an apology on the way out which brought a smile to her face.

After taking a sip of coffee, she tackled the unopened letters. Thankfully, there were only a few, and then she sat and sifted through the rest of the dross that had built up in her absence.

Bob reappeared ten minutes later and asked, "Are you still speaking to me?"

"Only just. I know I left you in the lurch. You did your best. That's all a boss can ask for, partner."

"You know I can't stand paperwork at the best of times."

"That much has been evident over the years. Are the rest of the team here yet?"

"All present and correct, boss."

"I'll be out in a minute or two."

Bob left her finishing up sorting the post into the relevant piles, according to their urgency, and then she booted up her computer. However, when she saw how many emails were waiting for her, she swiftly regretted her decision and shut it down again.

I'll deal with the actual post this morning and see about tackling that lot this afternoon. I'll be in need of sustenance by the time the end of my shift comes around, and Doreen's casserole will be the medicine I need to recover and start all over again tomorrow.

She left her chores and stepped into the incident room ten minutes later. The team all made a huge fuss over her. A large lump formed in her throat and she retreated into her office not long after.

"That was tough for you, wasn't it?" Bob asked. He deposited yet another coffee on her desk.

"Thanks. Yes, harder than I ever thought it would be."

"I've told them to tone it down a bit and to act normal. I hope it helps."

"Thanks, Bob. It's going to take a few days to settle back into things. It seems like I've been off for months, not just a week."

The phone rang on her desk. Sam answered it, again with anxiety gushing through her veins, while Bob lingered in the doorway. "Hello. DI Sam Cobbs. How can I help?"

"Sam, it's Des Markham, glad to hear you're back at work. Are you up for coming out to see me?"

"See you? Where? At a crime scene?"

"Yes. I'm at a cottage, or what's left of one, out at Bridekirk."

"I think I know it. I'll need to search for it on the satnav. Anything else you want to tell me?"

"Not really. I'll see you soon. Look out for Fell View Cottage. It's down a dirt track, be careful not to miss it."

"We'll do our best. We're leaving now, so expect to see us shortly." Sam shot out of her chair. "Des needs us to attend a crime scene, are you up for it?"

"More to the point, are you?" Bob asked.

"Let's put things into perspective here. I could spend my day trawling through this dross, going out of my mind, or… I could attend an urgent crime scene… It's a no-brainer to me."

"You might have a point there."

They tore through the incident room and down the stairs.

Outside the main entrance, Sam halted and faced her partner. "All right if we take your car? I wouldn't feel comfortable showing up at a crime scene in a loan car."

"Fine with me. In that case, I'll leave you to sort out the satnav."

"Thanks. I'll do my best. I always seem to have problems inputting information into yours."

He tutted. "I'll do it before we set off."

ONCE THEY REACHED the small village it took them a few minutes to find the dirt track the pathologist had mentioned. The scenery en route was breathtaking. Being a designated driver all the time, she never usually got the thrill of admiring her surroundings.

"I wonder what this is all about," Sam said.

"I have a feeling we're going to find out soon enough. Here's Des now. I'm going to have to park here, blocking the track."

"I don't see any other houses around, and there's only SOCO and Des here, so it shouldn't matter, not really."

They left the car. Des acknowledged their arrival with a curt nod. He was busy issuing instructions to one of the SOCO techs.

Once he'd finished, he turned his attention to Sam and Bob. "Hi, guys. First of all, I want to pass on my condolences, Sam. I wanted to give you a call last week but, in all honesty, I couldn't pluck up the courage to ring you."

Sam batted away the apology with a flick of her wrist. "It's fine. I appreciate the thought. Rather than dwell on the incident, I want to throw myself into my work, if it's all the same to you?"

"No problem. Right, as you can see, the cottage has burnt down. At first the fire investigator put the fire down to an accident, however, once he discovered the injuries of the victims, he soon changed his mind. I must say, I'm inclined to agree with him."

"What are you saying, that the victims were murdered and the fire was intentionally set to cover up the fact?"

Des peered over his shoulder at the remains of the building. "That's it."

"What type of injuries?" Sam asked. She followed his gaze and shook her head. "Thatched, was it?"

"I believe so. As to the injuries sustained, we're talking limbs being sliced off and a slit throat to one victim."

"Ah, that makes sense. I wondered if the collapsing building might have caused some of the injuries."

"The thought crossed my mind but, ah yes, I forgot to mention we've got evidence of the victims possibly being bound with rope as well."

"Okay, that sheds a different light on things. When did the fire happen, any idea?"

"Saturday. That's when the fire brigade attended the scene. The fire investigator worked over the weekend once it was safe for him to enter the cottage, and he called me in first thing this morning to get my opinion. He pointed out the evidence he had discovered and asked for my professional opinion. We're in the process of doing the necessary to preserve what's left of the bodies."

"Do we know if the victims were the owners?"

"No idea, sorry. That's down to you to find out. There is a car parked on the grass verge. You might want to try and trace the victims that way, at least, that's where I would start."

"Bob, do you want to do the necessary? Ring the station, see what they can find out from the plate number. Claire should be able to give us a heads-up on it virtually straight away."

"On it," Bob replied. He walked over to the car with his phone in his hand.

"We didn't notice any other properties around on our way here, did you?" Sam asked.

"No, although I wasn't looking at the time. There might be another property further down the track. Might be worth a punt."

"Who called the brigade, any idea?"

"Again, that's probably something you'll need to find out for yourself. I'm guessing it was someone in the vicinity. Maybe a hill walker saw the smoke and reported it."

"Possibly. Perhaps the murderer rang nine-nine-nine themselves."

"You might be on to something there. Maybe they hung around until the fire went too far and then called it in."

Sam nodded, and Bob rejoined them.

"Any luck?" she asked.

"The car is registered to a Daniel Mansell from Coventry," Bob confirmed.

"So he's a holidaymaker. Could be either a rental property or a second home. We're going to need to find that out, Bob." Sam withdrew her phone and entered *Fell View Cottage* into the search engine. It was registered on a couple of the national sites. Further digging produced the name of a rental agent in the local area, just up the road. "I've got it. It'll be a start. We'll begin the investigation there."

"What about the relatives of the deceased?" Bob asked.

"Maybe the agency will have next of kin details on file. Do you need us for anything else, Des?"

"Nope, you're free to go." He grinned and turned his back on them.

"I'm going to need to reverse all the way back up the

lane," Bob complained. "I can't see anywhere for us to make a U-turn around here."

"How are your reversing skills?"

"Average. Yours?"

"I'd oblige, but only in my car, so you're on your own, matey."

"Figures."

THEY ARRIVED at Valley Rentals around fifteen minutes later.

Sam showed her ID to the blonde who was sitting at the desk closest to the front door. "DI Sam Cobbs. Is the manager around, please?"

"Oh, yes, of course. I'll get Pat for you now." She left the desk and trotted across the room to a door on the other side. "Sorry to trouble you, Pat. The police are here to see you."

"Police? Okay, Annie, tell them I'll be right out."

A woman in her fifties, smartly dressed in a grey pinstriped skirt suit and red blouse, came out of the office a few seconds later. "Hello, I'm Pat O'Brien. You wanted to see me?"

"Would you mind if we did this in private, Mrs O'Brien?"

"It's Miss. You'd better come into my office. Can I offer you a tea or coffee?"

"We're fine, thanks all the same."

"Very well." Pat led the way back to her office and instructed Sam and Bob to take a seat opposite her.

The office was tidy, and there wasn't a thing out of place on the woman's desk. Sam couldn't help but feel a stab of envy rising.

Once they were all seated, Pat asked, "Sorry to be so blunt, but I've never had a visit from the police before. Can you tell me why you're here? Has someone made a complaint about the firm?"

"No, it's nothing like that. We were called to a crime scene earlier and wondered if you'd be able to help us with our enquiries."

Pat's brow wrinkled. "How so?"

"We believe a cottage on your books was destroyed by a fire over the weekend."

Pat gasped and shook her head. She tapped her keyboard to bring her screen to life. "Do you have the name of the cottage?"

"Fell View."

"Oh my. I know it well, it's one of the nicer cottages we rent out. It's just undergone recent renovations. How did the fire start? Don't tell me it was faulty electrics?"

"We're not certain of the facts at this stage. There was a car registered to a David Mansell outside the cottage. We're assuming he was renting it. Can you confirm this?"

"Let me see what I can find out for you on the booking system. You'll have to bear with me, it's all new and takes a while to navigate, unlike the old system. I still can't believe this has happened. I've never experienced anything as tragic as this before and I've been running this business for over twenty years. Here it is. Damn, they only arrived on Saturday. Annie welcomed them to the cottage. We try to personally welcome as many of our guests as possible, time permitting, of course. It's a lot easier at this time of the year."

"What sort of details do you hold for your clients on the system? Would you have a next of kin registered?"

"Yes, I always insist on taking those details, you never know when you might need them, especially when people like to go off hill walking."

"I agree. It can be a dangerous activity to indulge in. Would it be possible for you to give us the details of the next of kin? Can you also tell us how many people were staying in the cottage at the time? I'll also need the owner's details, too. Sorry if that's going to cause you a lot of work."

"It shouldn't do, it should all be here. Let me call Annie in to lend a hand." She left her seat and opened the door. "Annie, do you have a second?"

The blonde, Sam had initially spoken to, entered the room. "Can I help, Pat?"

"Distressing news, dear. One of our cottages… what am I saying? Let me correct that: there's been a fire, and possibly some of our clients have perished in the flames."

"No way. How dreadful. Which cottage?"

"Fell View. I know it's one of your favourites."

Annie's eyes widened, and she shook her head. "Goodness me. The clients renting it were such a nice couple, too. Are you sure they're dead? Maybe they were out when the fire started?" The younger woman directed her questions at Sam.

"Two bodies were found in the debris."

"What do you need me to do, Pat?"

"The officers need the name of the homeowners and the next of kin for the people renting the cottage. Was it just the two of them staying there?"

"Yes, they were newlyweds. This was supposed to be their honeymoon. I'll get the details for you, don't worry, Pat. It'll take me a few minutes."

"Use my computer. There's a notebook in the top left-hand drawer."

Annie went over to the desk and scrolled through a number of screens. She jotted down the details and handed them to Sam. "There you go. Do you need anything else while I have the file up on the screen?"

"When was the cottage last rented out?"

Annie scrolled again. "Two weeks ago. Damn, it's booked out a few more times this month. Do you want me to cancel those, Pat?"

"Offer the clients an alternative. Hopefully, they'll understand our predicament and won't want to cancel on us completely. Let me know how you get on." Pat leant on the desk and sighed. "I hope something as devastating as this doesn't affect our business. It's been a tough couple of years and, well, no, I'm not going there, you don't want to hear about all my gripes."

Frowning, Sam replied, "I thought staycations were all the rage after the lockdown."

"Yes and no. I really don't want to come across as selfish. Let's end the conversation there. Is there anything else you need from me?"

"I can't think of anything at this moment. I'll be in touch if I need any further information. You've saved us a lot of trouble, supplying us with these details. We appreciate your assistance."

"We aim to please. I think it's horrendous that two people have lost their lives on their honeymoon. That traumatic knowledge will remain with me until the day I die. Sorry if that sounds too dramatic, it's just that we pride ourselves on ensuring our clients have their best holidays ever in one of our cottages. Isn't that right, Annie?"

"I agree. I'm heartbroken, they were such a lovely couple, you could tell how much they adored each other by the way they looked at one another. They were relatively young, too, with their whole lives still ahead of them."

"All right, Annie. Don't go getting upset. Run along now and get those future bookings rearranged and report back to me once you've completed the task. Try and keep the conversation as upbeat as you can."

Annie's brow knitted. "Are you sure, Pat? Won't the clients think that's a tad strange?"

"Good grief, only if you tell them the true reason behind rearranging their booking. You can mention the fire, but don't, I repeat *don't,* go informing them that two holiday-makers lost their lives in the blaze. We'd never get another booking if word got around."

Sam raised a finger to interrupt their conversation. "Forgive me butting in, but in my opinion, your clients are bound to hear about the accident on the news." *Actually, they're going to hear a lot more than that when the truth about the fire is revealed through the media. There are certain journalists I know who will jump all over this case and milk it for what they can get out of it if the fact that the deaths are suspicious comes to light.* But Sam kept her lips sealed about that for now. Until the cause of death had been verified by the pathologist, there was no way she'd be giving any hints in that department, either now or in the near future.

"You're right. Bugger, what a dilemma we have on our hands. Damned if we do and equally damned if we keep schtum," Pat agreed.

"It's a tough one for you to deal with, I don't envy you."

"Annie, I'll leave the decision in your capable hands. I'm sure you can dig into that smart brain of yours and come up with a reasonable explanation that is as far removed from the truth as we are from the M25."

Annie snorted. "Leave it with me, Pat. I'll see what I can come up with." The younger woman breezed out of the room, giving Sam and Bob a cursory smile and nod on the way out.

"She seems very efficient. Always good having staff you can rely on," Sam said once the door was closed.

"She has her moments. I'm fortunate that she has the same vision as me for the business. The lady who I employed before Annie was such hard work. Very negative and stuck her oar in where it wasn't wanted most days. She was older, though. I suppose she thought she was more experienced than she really was. That's why I chose someone younger to fill her shoes. Anyway, that's by the by. What happens now with your investigation? Will we be in trouble? Before you answer that, I'd like to assure you that we ensure all our properties are up to standard before we take them on. We also chase insurance documents up as a yearly task, so we're on the ball there, as well."

"That's reassuring. I'm glad you're thorough. As far as the investigation goes, we'll need to get in touch with the next of kin to tell them about the fatalities. Not ideal to do it over the phone. I'll have to pass the details over to the local police to deal with."

Pat returned to her chair and ran a hand over her face. "Such a daunting task. What dreadful news to receive. I can't imagine how the next of kin will take it. Shocking, it is, truly shocking."

"We'll leave it there then. Should we have any further questions in the next few days, we'll get in touch."

Pat removed a card from the plastic container on her desk and slid it towards Sam. In turn, she removed one of her own from her pocket and sent it in the opposite direction, then stood, ready to leave. Pat showed them out of the office and held the front door open for them. There, she hesitated in offering her hand to shake.

Sam smiled. "We'll refrain, if you don't mind. In light of what we've just been through with the pandemic."

"Of course. I'm of the same opinion in all honesty. Good luck with your investigation. Please don't hesitate to call if you need further assistance from us."

"We'll be sure to get in touch should the need arise. What you've supplied so far will give us an excellent foundation to get us up and running."

"My pleasure."

Sam and Bob left and jumped in the car.

"Where to now?" Bob asked.

"We need to get back to the station and call the next of kin, not a job I'm relishing at all."

"What's the protocol on this? Do you call the family directly or would you need to go through the force in the relevant area to break the news?"

"What I'm going to do is cover my back and ring the local force before I contact the families. They should be made aware of the investigation anyway. I know if something like this happened elsewhere and it affected residents from our area, I would want to know."

"Yeah, I'd feel the same way. Will it be worth asking the local plod to do some background checks just in case?"

Sam tapped the side of her nose and winked at him. "Now we're thinking along the same lines, partner. It seems strange that the couple should get murdered on the same day they arrive. Maybe the killer followed them all the way up here, confronted them about something, and then decided to do the deed here rather than back in their own area."

"Yeah, I get that. Umm... mind if I speak openly with you?"

Sam frowned and chewed on her lip. "You don't usually have to ask before you jump in with your size tens. What's up?"

Bob cleared his throat. "It's just that I felt a slight hesitancy on your part back there, as if you were holding back a little. Were you?"

Sam shook her head. "I don't think so. Maybe it's a case of you reading things into it that just aren't there."

"Perhaps you're right, and if that's the case, then forgive me for being overly concerned about you."

"I'm fine. I'll let you know if things start to overwhelm me. At the moment, I'm more perplexed about the case than anything else."

"I just thought… well, you know, what with it being a fire and all…"

"Ah, I'm with you now. Why do you have to go ten times around the block instead of coming right out with it and saying what's on your mind?"

"Blimey, I can never get it right, can I? Because you'd probably call me an insensitive bastard, that's why."

Sam chuckled and motioned for him to start the car. "I wouldn't. Come on, chauffeur for the day, we'd better get back to the station."

"Talking of which, what's happening about your car? Any news on that front?"

"You know what insurances are like, they love nothing more than making you jump through hoops before they shell out any funds due. I'm not bothered about it for now, I have too many other things occupying my mind."

"Like the funeral?" he asked, barely above a whisper.

"Yep. Chris's parents arrived a few days ago. So far, they've kept their interference to a minimum, but I'm getting the sense that things are about to get antsy soon."

"Good luck with that one. I'm guessing another few days and Chris's funeral wouldn't have been on your shoulders."

"Correct. With the divorce finalised, I would no longer have been his next of kin. Instead, and on top of everything else my dearly departed estranged husband heaped on my shoulders, I got burdened with the expense of arranging the funeral and all that entails."

"So bloody wrong on so many levels. Especially the way he went out and the devastation he caused… I'm sorry, you don't want to be reminded about that. Forget I brought it up."

Sam patted his leg. "I'm not made of delicate porcelain, you're allowed to bring up any subject with me, you know that."

"I know, but I'm also cautious about trampling all over your emotions, too. In my ham-fisted way, what I'm trying to tell you is that if you need any help, I'm here for you. All you have to do is ask."

"I appreciate it, partner. I'm back at work for a reason, I was going out of my mind at home, although I loved being around Sonny all day. He was a great source of comfort to me in the darker moments."

"Hey, you're not telling me that you're blaming yourself for what Chris did, are you?"

"No, not in the slightest, although I'm bound to wonder if me having a go at him was the cause of tipping him over the edge."

"No way! You need to crush that idea right away. Read my lips: he must have been unhinged in the first place, you were not to blame for him taking his own life, got that?"

Sadness swept over her, and a lump settled in her throat. She nodded, unable to speak.

Bob twisted in his seat and placed a hand on her forearm. "Sorry, that was a bit strong, but you get my drift. There's no way you should be feeling guilty about what's taken place, you hear me?"

Tears misted her eyes, and she nodded. "It's the rest of it I'm struggling to deal with." She inhaled a deep breath and waved a hand. "I don't want to speak about it any more, Bob."

His mouth turned down at the sides, and he started the engine. "I'm here if you need me. That's the end of it as far as I'm concerned."

"You're one in a million, Bob Jones. Don't let anyone tell you differently either."

"I'll send them your way if they try and argue with me, how about that?"

Sam smiled, feeling more like her old self. It was good to be back, working alongside Bob. He was down to earth, a pain in the arse at times on certain issues, but a good egg all the same whose heart was in the right place. "Thanks. Let's get this show on the road, eh?"

"Your wish is my command." He revved the engine and pulled into a gap in the traffic.

CHAPTER 3

Back at the station, and with another cup of coffee to hand, Sam settled behind her desk and searched for the relevant number. She spoke to someone at the control centre who gave her a direct line for a detective based at the police station in the Mansells' town.

"Detective Inspector Alan Wareing, how may I help?"

"Ah yes, I'm hoping you can. I'm DI Sam Cobbs of the Cumbrian Constabulary. Do you have five minutes for a chat?"

"It depends on what it's in connection with, Inspector."

"A murder inquiry."

"You've managed to grab my attention. Go on."

Sam explained the situation to him, giving him every detail they had uncovered so far, which in truth, didn't amount to much.

"I see. And you're suspecting foul play from this end, is that it?"

Sam shrugged as if he were in the room with her. "It's hard to say. I was wondering if you'd be willing to do some digging at that end for me, or if you'd deem that to be a waste of your time."

"Why not?"

"Thanks, that would be a great help."

"What sort of details were you after?"

"We need to know if there's anything in either Daniel or Tara's background. I know very little about them as yet, apart from what was on their registration form. Apparently, he was an insurance rep and she was a nurse. Just basic details, the rental agency didn't go into specifics on their forms."

"Why don't you leave it with me for a few days and I'll get back to you?"

"That would be perfect. Umm… there's the next of kin to be informed, can your lot do it at your end?"

"Er… I'll pass it over to uniform. I avoid that side of things like the plague. I can give you a call back once the task has been carried out. That leaves you open to ring the parents then."

"That would be great. Speak to you soon."

Sam whizzed through her emails and it wasn't long before Alan called her back.

"All done. You're good to go," he told her, chirpier than she'd anticipated.

"That was quick. Thanks." Sam ended the call and took a couple of sips from her mug. Then she picked up the phone once more and dialled the first number which belonged to Elizabeth Mansell, Daniel's mother.

"Hello."

"Mrs Mansell? I'm Detective Inspector Sam Cobbs of the Cumbrian Constabulary. One of my colleagues down there has just visited you."

Mrs Mansell sniffled. "That's correct. What do you want?"

"I'm so sorry for your loss. I wanted to fill you in on a few details, if I may. I'm not really sure what you've been told about your son's death."

"They died in a fire." Mrs Mansell sobbed then blew her nose. "I'm sorry, I'm so upset."

"Of course you are, that's totally understandable. Are you up to talking or should I call back another time?"

"Yes, I mean, no. I don't know. What do you want to tell me?"

"When the fire investigator showed up to examine the cause of the fire, he called in the local pathologist to assess the scene. Together, they determined it to be a crime scene."

"I don't understand. What are you saying?"

"That we believe the fire was probably deliberately started."

Mrs Mansell gasped and then burst into tears again. "This can't be happening. I only lost Daniel's father two months ago from a heart attack, and now you're telling me that my son and his beautiful wife have been... killed?"

"Yes, I'm truly sorry for your loss."

"I'm coming up there. I have to. But how will I get there? I don't drive. Is there a train service that reaches that far up? I haven't got a clue."

"There is a very efficient service, I believe. Are you sure you want to make the trek?"

"Absolutely. I'll pack up a bag and come right up," she said, full of determination. "Oh my, I'm not thinking straight, I can't do that as I have a hospital appointment that I need to attend. I'm due to have hip surgery next month and I need to go for a pre-op meeting with the consultant. I'm sorry, you didn't need to hear that. I'm talking nonsense, it must be the shock."

"That's totally understandable. If you want to come up in the next few days, then so be it. Are you sure you're going to be all right?"

"I doubt if I'll ever be all right again. He was my only child. You don't expect to outlive your children, do you?"

"No, you don't. I'll give you my number, should you need to contact me." Sam did just that. "I'm going to need to speak with Tara's parents now."

"Poor Ian and Yvonne will be as distraught as I am to hear the news. Wait, do you know what caused the fire? You didn't say, did you?"

"I didn't. We're awaiting the results from the forensics team, but we suspect the fire wasn't an accident."

"But why would someone do that? And to my son and his wife? Why? None of this is making any sense to me at all."

"I'm sorry, that's all I can share with you at this time."

"I'm not happy about that, but there is little I can do about it, for now."

"I'll be in touch soon. Again, I'm sorry for your loss."

"Thank you for ringing me. I'll get up there soon."

"Take care of yourself."

The line went dead. Sam took another couple of sips of coffee to calm her nerves and then dialled the second number.

A woman answered the phone, sounding upset. "Hello. Yvonne Knox. Who is this?"

"Hello, Mrs Knox, this is DI Sam Cobbs of the Cumbrian Constabulary. Is it convenient to have a chat with you?"

"Not really. I've just been delivered the most shocking news. Wait, Cumbria police, you said? Can you tell me how my daughter died?"

"Yes, this is a follow-up call to the news you've been given. I'm sorry I couldn't be there when you heard about your daughter's death."

"How did it happen?"

"We believe the fire was deliberately started and are treating it as a murder inquiry."

The line remained silent.

"Mrs Knox, are you all right?"

"Yes. What do you expect me to say to that?" A harsh breath escaped the woman as though she had sat down. "When did this happen? I've tried calling them over the weekend and got no response from either of their phones. I thought they might have been in a bad reception area. Oh my God!"

"We believe it occurred on Saturday evening. We've had a chat with the rental agency this morning, they gave me your details. One of the women at the agency greeted Tara and Daniel at the cottage and left not long after. We believe someone might have been watching the cottage and..."

"Wait... are you telling me they were specifically targeted? Don't keep things from me, Inspector, I'm a nurse. I get to see and hear about all sorts in my line of work."

"Yes, we believe that to be the case."

"Oh God. This is the worst news possible to hear at this time. Daniel has just lost his father, and my husband is going through cancer treatment right now."

"That's terrible. I'm so sorry. All I can do is assure you that we will get to the bottom of this and ensure you get the justice you all deserve."

"I should hope so. I'll have a word with my husband. He's bound to want to come up there, you know, be there on site while the investigation is underway. I'll book a week's holiday that was due to me, today. Expect us soon, Inspector."

"I look forward to meeting you in person. Please take care of yourself in the meantime. Sending you my best wishes."

"Thank you."

Sam ended the call with tears in her eyes, her own emotions swelling, despite her best efforts to keep them contained.

Bob knocked on the door to check on her around ten minutes later. By that time, she thought she had recovered sufficiently enough to carry on, but the look of concern on her partner's face, told her differently. She raised a hand as he opened his mouth to speak. "Don't say it."

"Okay, I won't. But if all this is too much for you then you need to lighten your load, Sam. I'm here, you only have to shout if you need to delegate some jobs to me."

"I'm coping fine. It's awkward speaking to people over the phone when they've just been told the devastating news, that's all. How's it going out there?"

"I brought the team up to speed with what we were confronted with. They're all gutted but determined to catch the killer. I took a punt and started searching the CCTV in an attempt to locate the Lexus on its way to the cottage."

"Good shout. I was going to suggest the same. Maybe they had a run-in with someone on the journey up here who got narked and followed them to the cottage. As soon as they saw Annie leave, that's when they made their move."

"A distinct possibility," Bob agreed. "What about the next of kin? I'm not going to ask how they took the news because that would be just plain stupid."

A smile strained on Sam's lips. "The parents are on their way up here. We'll see how that works out. The news came as a shock, obviously. No one expects to hear such awful news when your children are supposed to be on holiday, enjoying themselves."

"There is that. I know I'd be shocked and angry in their shoes."

"I also contacted an inspector in the Coventry area, explained the situation to him and asked him to do some digging for us. He's going to drop by the couple's places of work and carry out the usual background checks and get back to me in the next few days. Apart from that, there's very little else we can do. There's no point conducting house-to-house enquiries what with the cottage being so remote. The frustrating part is that the couple were tourists in the area. You know how much of our job centres around questioning the family and friends, even work colleagues, in an attempt to put all the pieces of a puzzle together. That has been taken from us. Again, was that intentional? Were the couple targeted because they were obvious holidaymakers, or is there something far more sinister going on here? If there is, where the hell do we start looking for clues?"

"Exactly. I can tell how frustrated you're getting already. None of this is our fault, all we can do is our best in any given situation. We'll work harder, if that's what it takes, put in longer hours, if it's needed. It's what we do to bring a criminal down."

Sam nodded. "I'm glad we're on the same page on this one, Bob. Shit, I was supposed to visit the boss first thing this morning and I forgot."

Bob shrugged. "He can't be that bothered, otherwise he would have chased you up by now."

"True. I'd better pop along and see him all the same. Not something I'm relishing, the level of frustration jarring me at present."

"Don't let him bully you, not that you would anyway."

"Thanks for the advice. I'll be back soon, I hope." Sam left her desk and followed Bob out of the office. She trotted along the corridor to visit DCI Armstrong. Heidi, his secretary, gave her a sympathetic smile when she entered the room.

"Hi, how are you, Inspector Cobbs? I was saddened to hear the news."

"Thanks, Heidi. It was a shock at the time. I'm doing well now. It slipped my mind to drop in and see the boss first thing. Is he available for a quick chinwag now?"

Heidi checked the phone to see if his line was free. "I'd better ask him. I won't be long." She left her seat and rapped her knuckles on the door to her left. After Armstrong bellowed for her to enter, she poked her head into the room. "Sorry to disturb you, sir. I have DI Cobbs wanting a quick chat with you, if you're free."

"Thanks, Heidi. I can spare ten minutes. Send her in."

Heidi pushed the door open and gestured for Sam to go in.

"Thanks, Heidi," she whispered as she passed.

"Ah, Sam. Come in. Let's get the tough part out of the way first. I was sorry and appalled to learn what you've been through. How are you feeling now?"

"I'm okay, sir. Coping better than I expected."

"You were still married at the time of Chris's death, weren't you?"

"That's correct. So yes, organising his funeral is down to me."

He tutted and shook his head. "My, oh, my, what an utterly dreadful situation to find yourself in. If there is anything I can do to help, you only have to ask. I mean it, Sam, don't hold back and, more importantly, don't bottle things up, it's the worst thing you can do. Take it from someone who has lost a loved one recently."

Sam inclined her head and frowned. "You have? I wasn't aware of that, sir. May I ask who?"

"I prefer not to bring my personal life to work, I flick a switch. I suppose we're all like that really, aren't we? Otherwise, you wouldn't have come back to work so soon after that appalling… umm, are we calling it an accident?"

"It's not something I've really thought about. *Accident* doesn't really cut it in my eyes, considering the devastation it caused."

"I heard there were others involved. Do you want to speak about that, or is it still too raw for you?"

"The level of rawness is pretty high right now. What I will tell you, and I hope I don't sound too much like a drama queen when I say that my life imploded the night Chris chose to take his own life. For several reasons, he damaged me in ways I never thought possible. Ugh... I do sound like a drama queen, I'm sorry."

"Don't be silly. I can imagine, or should I say I can't, not really. Are you sure you're up to being back at work? We could get by for another week or so without you. Not that I'm trying to get rid of you." He offered a rare smile.

"Had you said that to me yesterday, I would have jumped at the chance to have remained at home. I still have lots of things to arrange for the funeral."

"So what's changed?"

"We've taken on an intriguing, yet frustrating case, which I'm hoping will successfully take my mind off my own problems."

"Care to tell me about the case?"

Sam sighed and gave him a rough outline. He steepled his fingers and bounced in his executive chair as he listened.

"Oh heck," he said. "Not what I was expecting to hear at all. Are there any clues left, or did the fire destroy everything? I'm surmising the latter."

"That's the frustrating part. Maybe we're after a crafty killer who knows the ins and outs of how to commit the perfect crime."

"It wouldn't be the first time, would it?"

"Nope, although I have to say, criminals generally slip up along the way, leading to their capture."

"Let's hope that's the case on this one. I take it the next of kin have been informed?"

Sam sighed. "They have. They're making arrangements to come up here."

"Ouch, I hope they don't get in the way when they arrive."

"Me, too. I'll need to keep my distance if they try to, and that's bound to cause some hassle."

"And you want me to cover your back?"

Sam grinned. "Isn't that your job?"

They both laughed.

"It has been said on occasion, yes. I'll do what's necessary in order for you to concentrate all your efforts on the investigation. How did the team cope in your absence, any concerns there?"

"Not from what I can tell. Bob's pretty good at handling the team when I'm not around, although I wouldn't say that too loudly in his presence, his head is big enough as it is."

"You've built an exceptional team around you over the years, they're a credit to you. I'm guilty of not praising you and your team enough, so slapped wrist for me."

"At least you don't come down heavily on us like a lot of DCIs do."

"I try not to. I'm probably as guilty as anyone of losing my rag now and again, but then, I'm like you in that respect, we always expect professionalism at all times, don't we?"

"Holding my hand up to that one."

"Okay, I'm satisfied that you've made the right decision coming back into the fold. If you need to run anything past me regarding the case, if any self-doubts hamper you during the investigation, don't hesitate to knock on my door."

"Thanks, sir. I'll bear it in mind. I'll also keep you informed at regular intervals how the case is going."

"Do that. I must say, from what you've said about it so far, I don't envy your position."

"These cases are sent to try us. What doesn't beat us to a pulp makes us stronger, apparently. So I've been told."

DCI Armstrong smirked. "Let's hope you're not ground to mush at the end of it. Don't suffer in silence, Sam, I mean it. Shout if you need me to contribute."

"I will, I promise. Permission to get back to it now, sir?"

He sat upright and gave a brief nod. "Permission granted. I send you out of here with my best wishes for a much brighter future, Sam."

Tears threatened again as she got to her feet. She gave a slight cough to clear her throat of the emotion stuck there. "You're very kind."

Sam reached the door and turned when the chief said, "And if you need any time off to deal with the arrangements, just take it. I know you're not the type to swing the lead."

"Again, thank you, sir. I won't let you down."

"Well, you never have in the past, so I recognise that as a truthful statement."

She smiled and left the room.

Heidi glanced up from her keyboard and beamed at her. "How did it go? He's a pussycat once you get to know him."

"He is indeed. Very supportive, I couldn't ask for a more understanding boss."

Heidi winked. "He's misunderstood by a lot of people. It takes something such as what you're going through for his true colours to shine through." She placed a finger to her lips. "Shh... I didn't tell you that."

"Your secret is safe with me. See you later."

"Have as good a day as possible, Inspector," Heidi said before Sam exited the outer office.

She stopped off for a quick wee on the way back to the incident room then rejoined the rest of the team, her spirits lifted because of the way the DCI had spoken to her. *One kind word can make such a difference to someone's life.*

"You seem brighter," Bob said, the second she entered the room.

"I feel it. It's great knowing you have your colleagues' support and that of your senior officer. Anyone want a coffee?"

A few tentative hands raised.

"I'll help you, boss," Claire offered. She pushed back her chair and joined Sam at the drinks station.

"Thanks, Claire. How are things with you? Is Scott busy?"

"He never stops, seven days a week."

"Sorry to hear that, love. He needs to spend more time with you and the kids. Pass that on for me, will you? Life's too short as it is. Tell him not to waste it working all the hours and missing out on family time."

Claire stared at the cups she was preparing and nodded. "I'll be sure to tell him, boss. I doubt if he'll listen, though."

"Seriously, you need to sit him down before it's too late. I don't wish to be maudlin, but pushing yourself to the limits daily helps no one in the end."

"I agree. If I start on about the time he's spending at work, he takes offence and we end up not talking for days. I find myself picking the battles I'm prepared to fight."

"Chin up, I'm sure he'll listen in the end. I know how stubborn some men can be."

"Ain't that the truth? I'll distribute the cups."

"You're a good 'un, Claire, I don't care what Bob says behind your back."

"What was that?" Bob demanded after hearing his name being mentioned.

"I was talking about you, not to you, partner."

He groaned and continued to search the screen ahead of him, with Liam by his side. Sam picked up two mugs and put them on the table next to Bob.

"How's it going?" she asked. Sam returned to pick up another mug and walked back to stand alongside her partner.

Bob pointed at the screen. "We've spotted the Lexus on a couple of ANPRs and now we're checking the CCTV cameras along the route. Nothing suspicious has shown up so far."

"Not what I wanted to hear. What about getting a close-up of the couple in the vehicle? How do they seem to you?"

Bob turned to look at her. "What are you suggesting? That all was not well between them and one of them killed the other before starting the fire? A murder-suicide?"

Sam held her empty hand up and shrugged. "It's not beyond the realms of possibility, is it?" She took a sip from her mug and observed the footage on the screen.

"It hasn't crossed my mind. I suppose we're going to be reliant on what the PM report tells us about the causes of death."

"That's going to be difficult, it's not like they can count on blood spatter evidence to lead them to come to any significant conclusions. I'll have a word with Des, plant the seed in his mind. He'll probably laugh off the idea initially. However, I believe it's something we should consider. How often do murderers cover their tracks by lighting fires?"

"That doesn't mean a thing."

"You have a point. It'll give us an angle to work on, at least. Claire, can you do me a favour? Check the system, see how many burglaries have occurred in the area of the crime scene in the past six months. No, make it twelve months."

"On it now, boss."

"Now you reckon it's a burglar turned killer?" Bob queried.

"Until something definite comes our way, then I think we need to open the door to every conceivable possibility, unless you can come up with an alternative idea."

Bob ran a hand over his face, and it snaked around the back of his neck. "Not right now."

"Yep, that's my point, it's far too early for us to disregard anything at this stage. We're running blind with this one. We don't have a clue about their relationship, if it was in any kind of trouble."

"Going by what Annie at the rental agency told us, she said they seemed a nice couple, newlyweds. Is it likely either one of them would resort to killing the other and then setting fire to the cottage?"

Sam tilted her head back and chewed on her bottom lip. "I'd forgotten all about that. Okay, scrub my idea for now."

"No, I think we need to keep it on the table," Bob advised. "Not that I'm trying to step on your toes or anything."

"You're not. Stop being so defensive, you know I'm always open to valid suggestions."

He nodded. "We've got the Lexus heading through the closest town here with no other cars following them. A vehicle comes out of the turning up ahead and follows them until the next turnoff, and that's it."

"Frustrating as it is, it means we don't have to waste our time trying to track down another vehicle." Sam's phone rang in her office. She left her mug on the desk behind her and sprinted to answer it. "DI Sam Cobbs. How may I help?"

"Hi, Sam. It's Alan Wareing from Coventry."

"Oh, hi. That was quick. I wasn't expecting you to get back to me for a few days. What's up?"

"What can I tell you? When I get the wind behind me, it's all systems go. I made some calls and thought I'd report back with my findings as I go along, if that's all right with you? Saves me wondering if I've told you something or not during our catchups."

"If that's the way you want to work things, it suits me. In that case, I'll give you my mobile number for when I'm out of the office." She gave it to him. "Dare I ask what you've managed to find out?"

"I spoke to Daniel's boss over the phone. I've made arrangements to see him in person later on today. He told me that Daniel had received a few threats lately from people he had refused to dish out payments to."

"Interesting. He's in the insurance industry, isn't he?"

"That's right. I'm not sure what it's like up there, but down here there have been a lot of scams with people slamming on brakes, shunting into the back of cars in order to get a substantial claim from the insurance company."

"I was on the wrong end of such an incident myself only last month. We caught the bastards. They're due up in court on that and several other charges in a few weeks."

He laughed. "Jesus, I bet that went down well with the scammers when you produced your ID."

"Not really. I kept them talking for a while, then they sped off. We captured them within twenty-four hours, so not too bad. Back to the investigation... How have these threats manifested?"

"One guy in particular showed up at the agency and collared Daniel after work. His boss, Colin, told me they had to call the police. I looked up the record—I'll send it through to you if you give me your email—and he was arrested on harassment charges, although ABH was also mentioned during the interview."

"Hmm... okay, that's something to go with, at least." She gave him her email address which he noted down. "Will you chase it up for me? Pay this guy a visit?"

"Already on the agenda for today. I thought I'd catch up with you first. I'll see what he has to say for himself, get an alibi and do the necessary with that."

"I'd check the ANPRs, see if his vehicle shows up as heading out of the area on Saturday as well. However, we've got access to local footage, and after going through it all, the victims' Lexus wasn't being followed from what we can tell."

"Still worth a check, though."

"I'd say so. Anything else for me?" she asked.

"Not yet. I haven't come across anything with Tara at all, but I'll keep digging. I thought I'd call around and have a word with their neighbours today as well."

"Good man. I really appreciate it. I feel so frustrated being so far away from the victims' hometown. Honestly, we haven't come across a single clue or piece of evidence at this end as yet. We're hoping that will surface once the PM report comes back. Until then, our hands are tied. We called at the agency who rented out the cottage; nothing untoward there either."

"Sounds like you're doing all the right things. I wouldn't stress too much about it just yet. I'll carry on digging for you. If you need anything else in the meantime, give me a shout."

"You're amazing. Thanks for your support, Alan. I'll personally buy you a pint when this is all over."

"You're in luck, I'm heading your way next spring, so I'll take you up on that offer."

"Have you visited The Lakes before?"

"I'm a frequent visitor. Or I was until my divorce was finalised."

"Ouch, sorry to hear that. Any kids involved?"

"No, thank goodness. It's fine. It was an amicable divorce, no anxiety or slanging matches involved. I think the job caused the initial cracks to develop in the first place, and over time, they widened until they became irreparable. It's the chance we take with our chosen career. I bet you get the same with your other half, don't you?"

Sam fell silent, her mind recapping the arguments she and Chris had gone through before he had walked out on her.

"Sam, are you still there?"

"I'm here. Umm… my marriage pretty much went the

same way as yours. I agree, it's like a snowball rolling down the highest mountain once it starts."

"Sorry to hear you've been through the same. Most coppers I know have problems with their marriage. Do you still get on with your ex? Or is the relationship now dead in the water?"

Sam cringed. "You're going to find out soon enough, so I might as well be the one to tell you. My ex-husband, although the divorce hadn't been finalised, it was going through the process… I digress. Anyway, Chris killed himself a little over a week ago."

"What the heck? Sending you my sincere condolences. Tell me to butt out if you like… was it because of the breakup?"

"Yes, well, actually, it was more because I refused to take him back once he moved in with his floozy and she'd given him the boot after a few weeks. I'd moved on by then and I suppose he couldn't handle me being with another man." Tears appeared for the umpteenth time that day. *Why in God's name am I opening up to a complete stranger?*

"Holy crap! I don't know what to say. I hope you're okay?"

"I'm getting there. As I'm still his legal next of kin, arranging the funeral has landed on my shoulders."

"Shit, and you're doing that as well as dealing with a huge case? I take my hat off to you. I mean it, Sam, you must be a hell of a detective if you're able to switch off from all that's going on around you at the moment."

"I have an excellent team here, and you've already proved your weight in gold. I can't thank you enough for what you're doing at your end for me."

"Seriously, it's no bother. I'm happy to pitch in. I hope that man of yours appreciates what an efficient and incredible woman he has on his hands."

"Umm... now that's another story I won't bore you with. I'm going to have to go, one of my team needs my attention."

"Hit a raw nerve, have I? It's fine, I know when I'm being given the brush-off. I'll be in touch soon. Take care."

"Thanks for being so understanding, Alan. Good luck."

CHAPTER 4

The following day started off pretty much the same as the previous one, with Sam bolting upright in bed after suffering the most horrific nightmare.

Will I ever be rid of these unwanted intrusions? What I need is to see a professional psychiatrist, or do I? I had one of those in my life, and look what happened.

She tore into the bathroom and dived under a hot shower, her face up to the rainfall showerhead. She let the water pour over her, washing away the remnants of sweat that had broken out during her disturbed sleep. It was an ideal way of refocusing her mind away from the destruction Chris had caused to her life the night he took his own.

Why? Why did he do it? Was he truly that desperate? Did I know him at all? Did I mistake his cries for help to satisfy my own appetite to get on with a life I had craved for, a happy and devoted life with Rhys, who had shown me nothing but respect and kindness?

Overwhelmed by the surging emotions once more, Sam completed her shower and the rest of her morning bathroom ritual and went back into the bedroom. Sonny was sitting in the middle of the room, his head tilted, whimpering.

She ran to him and got down on her knees. "I'm sorry, boy. Please forgive me. You must be desperate for the loo." Her usually structured routine had gone out of the window this past week or more. She had failed Sonny so many times lately that she found herself doubting whether she should ever had taken on the responsibility of having a dog, but no matter how many times the thought crossed her mind, she sent it packing immediately. There was no way she could ever part with him. No way! He was like a child to her. With Doreen and Vernon willing to look after him, she knew, if she failed him through her sheer forgetfulness, they would be there for Sonny, spoiling him, picking up the slack. She gave him a kiss on the nose and an extra hug.

"Come on, want to go in the garden, Son?"

He trotted over to the door and then thundered down the stairs. Sam took a more leisurely stroll down the staircase and opened the back door to find the ground wet and threatening black clouds overhead. "Make it quick, Sonny."

He relieved himself and ran back inside, straight into Sam's arms so she could dry him with the towel.

"You're a good lad." She topped up his water and food bowls then flew back upstairs to get ready. A ring at the doorbell interrupted her mid-flight. *What? You have to be kidding me, it's barely seven-thirty.* She turned, retraced her steps and removed the chain on the front door. Shock filled the next few seconds before her mind registered who was standing on her doorstep. "Mum! What the heck are you doing here at this time of the morning?"

Looking at Sam's wet hair, her mother said, "I'm so glad I didn't wake you. I've been sitting in the car, waiting for the lights to go on in the house. Give your mother a hug then."

Sam glanced down at the small suitcase lying at her

mother's feet. "Are you staying? Have I forgotten a conversation we had? I'm confused."

"No, it wasn't discussed. Well, your father and I talked it over and decided the best thing would be for me to just show up on your doorstep, first thing in the morning."

"Goodness me. This has totally knocked me for six. Why? Why are you here?"

"Because you need someone to help you with these damn funeral arrangements. The last time we spoke, I sensed you were overwhelmed and in dire need of help. I also think it was far too soon for you to entertain going back to work. What were you thinking?"

"Mum, I'm fine. What about your own job?"

Her mother was a maths teacher at a secondary school in Workington. Sudden guilt washed over her, not for the first time in the past week. She hadn't visited her parents in months, mainly due to work but also because of her fledgling relationship with Rhys, which had been all-consuming at the time.

"Are you going to invite me in?"

Sam collected the suitcase and stepped aside, allowing her mother to enter. "I'm sorry. I'm in shock right now."

"Of course you are, that's why I've come to be with you."

"No, not because of what's happened. I meant you turning up out of the blue like this has shaken me to the core, Mum. Your job?"

"Oh yes, you did ask. I've taken a week's holiday."

Sam inwardly groaned but made sure she kept her smile fixed in place. "Oh," was all she could summon up to say, her mind whirling. She had to get ready for work, stick to her already lax routine. What were the chances of that happening now that her mother had shown up?

"You pop up and get ready, and I'll knock you up some

breakfast. How does scrambled eggs on toast sound? Providing I can find the ingredients in your fridge."

"The bread is in the bin, and the eggs and milk are in the fridge. That sounds perfect. But, Mum, I have to go to work. I've taken too much time off already, and a new case landed on my desk yesterday which I'm keen to get back to today."

"Yes, yes, we'll discuss that over breakfast. Off you go."

Sonny sat beside her mother, waiting patiently to be petted. Sam's gaze dropped to her pooch, and her mother picked up on the hint and gave Sonny a quick stroke.

"He's no bother. Don't you ever feel guilty about leaving him all day?"

Sam raised an eyebrow. "Actually, all the time, however, the knowledge that he's in safe hands in my absence is a blessed relief at the end of the day."

"Ah, quite right, too. People shouldn't have dogs if they're out at work all day. What kind of life is that for this little chap?"

Rather than get into yet another heated, age-old argument about what a bad owner she was, Sam tutted and trudged up the stairs to get ready. She chuntered her disagreement at her mother turning up, uninvited, while she threw on her work clothes. What could she do? Kick her out? Send her packing again? Sam dried her hair, brushing it fiercely while her temper ebbed and flowed. She was grateful for the support her parents had given her over the past week, but this was out of order, coming here, unannounced.

What am I going to do now? I have to go to work, they're expecting me, and Doreen is also expecting me to drop Sonny off at her place before I leave. How is that going to look now, if I neglect to do it? Jesus, Mum, as much as I love you, I have my own life to lead, which most of the time, I do quite well. Yes, the wheels may have dropped off recently, but heck, everyone has to deal with these kinds of distractions now and again, don't they?

Two minutes later, Sam sucked in a large breath and descended the stairs once more. Her heart fluttered wildly at the sight of her mother's suitcase, sitting in the hallway.

"It's almost ready now, love. I don't think it's as good as usual but I'm working with strange equipment and a different stove to what I'm used to at home. We're all electric, and you're all gas. It's surprising what a difference it makes when you're using them."

"Don't worry, Mum. I'm grateful for whatever you've managed to knock up."

They sat at the table and tucked into their food. A subdued atmosphere descended. Sam struggled to strike up a conversation with her own mother, fearful she might put her foot in it and offend her.

Pushing her plate away, her mother placed her hands over her stomach and let out a satisfied breath. "It was rather delicious after all. Now then, where do we start?"

Sam finished her final mouthful and shoved her plate to the side then fidgeted in her seat. "I'm not sure what you're referring to, Mum." Although she had a rough idea in which direction the conversation would be steered next.

"Ah, avoidance tactics, I get it. Well, young lady, that might have worked with your father over the years, but never with me."

Sam placed an elbow on the table and cradled the side of her face in the palm of her hand. *Here goes. The conversation I've been dreading for the last nine days.*

"Don't go all huffy on me, you're a grown woman now, not a pouting, or should I say, sulking teenager. That is what you used to do, isn't it? Sulk? Again, rather than your father confronting or disciplining you, he decided on more than one occasion to let you have your way, which had disastrous results."

Sam raised her hand and stared at her mother. "I don't

remember that ever happening. I was a model child, you and Dad always demanded that we treated you with respect, and that's exactly what Crystal and I did, mostly."

Her mother raised a pointed finger. "There's the key word right there, *mostly*. Like I said, your father allowed you to get away with things I wouldn't have, because you were girls."

"I can't believe that for a moment."

"What about the time you ended up drunk when you were fifteen and your friends had to bring you home after you nearly drowned yourself in the River Derwent? And don't try and tell me I'm mistaken either. I've had to live with the image of you vomiting all over my brand-new leather sofa, for years."

Sam covered her eyes in shame and stayed silent, sensing there would be little to no point in denying the truth.

"Furthermore, you then went upstairs, without the bucket I insisted you take with you, and proceeded to vomit over your newly changed bed linen. Mortified, I was, not to mention absolutely horrified. Not because you were drunk and had grossly let yourself down—well, maybe a little because of that. No, it was mainly because you could barely stand up and yet you'd walked home in that state. Anything could have happened to you en route."

"That's unfair, because my friends were there. They wouldn't have allowed anything major to occur, hence fishing me out of the fast-flowing river by the scruff of my neck."

"Fast-flowing? That's the first I'm hearing about that. Good heavens. I dread to think what might have happened to you if your friends hadn't had your best interests at heart."

"It's done and dusted now. Why keep dredging up the past, Mum?"

"I'm doing it for a reason."

"Which is?"

"To highlight that despite how professional you are nowadays, that wasn't always the case. You have your vulnerable moments, and I believe there might be one on the cards at this time, hence my coming over here to be with you."

"And I've repeatedly told you over the phone, I'm handling it."

"But are you? There's no kidding the person who gave birth to you, Sam. Don't ever think that's possible, it's not. I can read you like a book. Now, are we going to talk about the elephant in the room?"

Sam frowned and shook her head. "I don't have a clue what you're on about." She crossed her fingers in her lap, hoping her mother wouldn't call her out on the lie she had just told.

"What about Rhys?"

Sam's gaze dropped to the table, and a burning sensation pricked her eyes.

"Sam, answer me. All I ever hear you mention is Chris... his departure from this world by his own hand, I might add. Not once have you openly told us about Rhys. Wasn't he supposed to be the new love of your life? He seemed to be pretty special to me, on the one occasion we met him."

"It's complicated, and I'd rather not discuss it, if you don't mind." Sam glanced up and noted the time on the clock. She gasped and pushed back her chair. "I have to go, I'm going to be late for work."

"You're not going anywhere, not until we've thrashed this out."

"You can't talk to me like that, mother or no mother. I left home years ago, Mum. I live and die by the mistakes I make in life."

"That's as may be, but it's often me or your father who has to pick up the pieces."

"I'm sorry if I've put you through the mill over the years

but I need you to back away on this one. I'm not ready to deal with the pain of losing him on top of burying my husband."

"Soon-to-be ex-husband. There are different emotions involved to each relationship, aren't there? Why did you have to complicate things? Why couldn't you have left it a few months before you got involved with this Rhys?"

Sam's head thrust forward. "What? By that, you mean that you're blaming me for the way Chris killed himself?"

"Now, did I say anything of the sort? No, I didn't. Don't go putting words into my mouth."

"I can't do this. Not here and definitely not now. I'm grateful you came, but there's no need. I'm better off at work. My mind focussing on a plethora of problems rather than dwelling on just one, planning Chris's funeral."

"I don't think you are. Ring in sick. Tell them it was a mistake you returning to work yesterday and that you need time out."

"I won't. I can't. I have a murder inquiry to deal with."

"*Delegate*. There's a novel word for you to get your head around."

"You used to tell me sarcasm was the lowest form of wit, Mother. How come it's acceptable for you to sink to that level and yet you refuse to allow others to do the same?"

Her mother's cheeks flushed beneath her glare.

"I… umm… I'm only looking out for you, Sam. If you choose to ignore my advice, then so be it."

"You can't just roll up here and start telling me how to run my life just because you think you know best. Up until now, I think even you will admit that I've done okay for myself over the years. What you're implying is that, one mishap, as grave as it is, has stopped me thinking for myself."

"Rubbish! Where the heck do you get that idea from? I'm

here to help. If me being here is going to cause problems between us then I might as well go home now."

"That's up to you, Mum. What I'm saying is that I have a life to lead and I refuse to drop everything just because you're telling me to. Support me by all means, but never come here and dictate to me how you think I should run my life."

The shock on her mother's face hurt Sam's heart. She regretted the tongue-lashing she'd set free but refused to apologise. Her mother had to realise there were boundaries that parents needed to observe in their children's lives just the same as there were if the roles were reversed.

Her mother's gaze dropped to her hand holding her mug. "I'm sorry. I'll have my drink and go home."

"I think it's for the best. I need to go to work now. Leave the washing-up, I'll do it when I return this evening. According to you, I have very little else to occupy my time, anyway."

"That's grossly unfair. I can't keep apologising to you, Sam. It was wrong of me to intrude, but I stand by what I've done, my intentions were good." Her mother rose from her chair.

Sam thought she was about to hug her but was disappointed when her mother cleared the plates and put them in the sink instead, then left the kitchen. Moments later, she slammed the front door on her way out. Sam raced into the lounge to see her mother putting the suitcase in the rear seat of her Merc and slipping behind the steering wheel. She hesitated and glanced back at the house. Sam was tempted to raise a hand and wave but at the last moment decided against it.

Her mother took the hint and drove away. Sam couldn't help it. Her emotions stripped bare, she sat on the sofa and cried. It was better to let it out than let it fester and spoil her mood for the rest of the day. Five minutes or so later, Sam visited the downstairs toilet and freshened up. She then dropped Sonny off at Doreen's.

Her neighbour opened the door.

Sam could tell there was something on her mind. "Morning, Doreen, everything all right?"

"I think so, dear. I was about to ask the same. Was that your mother I saw driving off? I didn't see her arrive last night."

"That's because she showed up this morning and I sent her packing."

"Oh dear, did you two have a row?"

"You could say that. Are you all right to take care of Sonny for me?" Sam's tone was choked with emotion.

"Of course. You never have to worry about that, Sam. Do you need to have a chat over a cuppa?"

Sam winced. "I'm sorry, I can't afford the time. I'm running late as it is, thanks to Mum appearing out of the blue."

"I understand. She's only concerned about you, dear. Like we all are."

"I know. I do appreciate it, but what people need to realise is that I left home at the age of eighteen and have been doing fairly well for myself ever since. She can't come around here dictating what she thinks I should do for the best."

"Absolutely. I'm sure she'll reflect on the way she approached the issue and call you later to apologise. Try not to let it spoil your day."

Sam smiled at Doreen who was one of the wisest women she had come across. It had taken her a while to realise just how wise, but that had become evident over the past week, during their frequent chats. Doreen had surprised her by holding interesting conversations about every topic under the sun and much more. In Sam's mind, there was no doubt about it, spending valuable time with her neighbour had definitely brought them closer together.

She handed over the bag containing Sonny's bits and bobs for the day and hugged Doreen. "You truly are a very special lady, and I know I always tell you this, but I don't think you realise how much I mean it. I'd be lost without you, supporting me the way you do."

Tears sparkled in Doreen's green eyes. "Get away with you. It's always a pleasure to help you out, Sam. I don't feel like you take advantage of me at all, and I love having Sonny here to keep me company."

"Just tell me if it all becomes too much for you. I know I say that a lot, but I never want to take advantage of you."

"You'll be the first to know. Now, shoo, be on your way, or you'll be getting your P45."

Sam cringed. "I could do without that added pressure, so thanks for that."

They both laughed.

Sam swooped to give Sonny a quick kiss on the nose and then kissed Doreen on the cheek. "Oops, maybe I should have done that the other way around."

"You reckon?" Doreen grinned. "Have a good day. Don't let what happened this morning get in the way, love."

"I won't. Thanks for caring, Doreen." Sam backed away and turned at the gate.

THE NEXT FEW days were spent mostly chasing the professionals involved in the case. With the deceased couple being visitors to the area, Sam felt the team's hands were exasperatingly tied. She even dropped by the mortuary to call in to see Des a few times to gee him up. She was still awaiting the results of the two post-mortems. That was just the way things were, after people perished in an arson attack. Alan Wareing had checked in with her a few times. Each call had ended with Sam's head dropping in despondency.

"What are we bloody missing, Bob?" she asked while they were taking an unexpected stroll along the river.

It had been Bob's suggestion to grab a sandwich away from the office. He could see how wound up Sam was becoming, cooped up within the four grey walls of the station. "I don't think it's a case of us missing anything, it's that nothing significant has come our way yet. Enough about work, how are you?"

"I'm fine."

He stopped and latched on to her forearm. "Seriously? You didn't appear to be fine this morning when you arrived. Not more bad news to deal with?"

"Not really. My mother showed up the other day and… well, it didn't go too well."

"Ouch! You don't want to be falling out with your parents, Sam, not at a time like this."

"I know. It's too late, I already have."

"What? Are you saying there's no way back from this?"

Sam stretched out her neck and rolled her head from side to side. "No, I'm not saying that at all, however, my mother needs to understand there are boundaries."

"Most parents can't comprehend that. We never grow up in their eyes. We're still their babes in arms. Their aim, no matter what age we are, is to protect us."

"You're right but… well, it's too late now."

He finished off the last of his roll and threw the wrapper in the nearest bin. "Yes, get in there. Sorry, I mean, it's never too late. You need to clear the air with her before it becomes too late."

"You're right. I'll give her a call once we get back to the

office. How are things with you? It's been a while since we've had a chance to catch up."

"Doing okay. My biggest concern lies with *you* at the moment."

"Why?"

"Because I'm constantly walking around on eggshells, scared to open my mouth in case you belt me."

"Belt you? When have I ever done that?"

"There's always a first time. The truth is, we're all worried about you, Sam. If you need a shoulder to cry on at any time, you know where I am."

"I don't," she said, sharper than intended.

"There's no need for that tone. You need to learn to accept that people care about you and lower your barriers now and again."

Sam paused and mulled over his suggestion. "I lowered my barriers a while back, and look where that got me."

"What are you talking about?"

Sam swallowed, trying to shift the lump that had developed in her throat. "Rhys. I had no intention of getting involved with anyone else… and then he came along."

"While you were still married, is that what this is all about? You feel guilty?"

"Yes. On so many levels. If I hadn't got involved with him, none of this would have happened. Chris wouldn't have felt the need to have gone to such lengths as to kill himself. Rhys would still be in my life, Benji would still… be alive…" She paused again, her nightmares coming to the fore and numbing her senses.

"Don't go there. I know how much Sonny means to you. Benji's death had nothing to do with you."

"Didn't it?" She turned to face him. "If Chris's car hadn't exploded and taken my car and Rhys's out with it, that poor dog would still be alive today."

"This is about so much more than that. Has Rhys been in touch since he moved out?"

She shook her head and wiped away the tears that had dripped onto her flushed cheeks. "No. He told me he needed time to come to terms with his loss. That dog meant everything to him, just as much as Sonny means to me."

Bob tutted and wrapped an arm around her shoulders. "People do crazy things where their pets are concerned. It pisses me off that he can treat you so badly. At a time when you need his compassion and support, he's gone and done the dirty on you. Sodding deserted you."

"Don't think badly of him. I understand why he left me. How could he be happy in that house with me, if every day he looked out of the window and was reminded of the raging inferno that took his dog's life?"

"Shit happens. We all have to deal with crap like this now and again. The first sign of trouble, and he hits the road? That ain't good enough in my opinion, maybe you're better off without him."

She stared long and hard at her hands and finally picked at a loose bit of skin around her thumb. "If you're right, then why do I feel so damn destroyed? As if all the joy I had ever possessed has been stripped from me? Why?"

"Because you're also grieving. Whether you like it or not, guilt is playing a major part in all of this. Chris was a jerk, you know my sentiments about the guy, but he used to be a major part of your life, at one time you worshipped him. Maybe you're clinging on to those emotions where you should be riled up about him dumping you instead. He left the marriage while you still loved him. Yes, you might have already met Rhys by then and your heart fluttered every time you saw him. But there's no escaping what that bastard Chris did to you. In your heart of hearts, you know I'm right, Sam.

This has to end before any real damage is done, up here." He jabbed at his temple.

"It's too late. I've lost everything. What is there to live for now?"

Bob held her face in his hands. His gaze holding hers, he whispered, "You dare give up on life and I'll kill you myself, you hear me?"

Sam smiled through her tears and removed his hands. She hugged him. He hugged her back, hard.

"You're an exceptional man, Bob Jones. Abigail doesn't know how special you are. Please, don't waste your energy on me, I'll get through this turmoil, eventually."

"I have no doubt you will. I'll make sure you don't drift off the rails again. If anything were to happen to you, where would that leave the team?"

"You'd cope under the guidance of another great inspector who would take my place."

Bob wrinkled his nose. "I doubt it. You're the best around, you just don't realise it."

"Get away with you. You can be such a creep when you want to be."

"I can? I thought sucking up to the boss was in my job description. You know what I would do in your circumstances?"

She raised her eyebrows and said, "Go on, surprise me."

"After work tonight, I would call in and see Rhys, see if you can't sort this all out with a heart to heart. He's a psychiatrist, for fuck's sake, he should recognise the chaos your emotions are in right now."

"I can't force him to speak to me. It was his decision to pack up and leave. Why should I plead with him to see me?"

"Because if you don't, the longer you leave it, the more irreparable the damage will be, too much to put right. Don't tell me the day he walked out you stopped loving him, because frankly, I won't believe you."

"Of course I didn't. But there's no way I'm about to storm into his office and demand that he comes back to me. He's grieving, too. Benji was a major part of his life, more than a dog, he was a family member, the child he'd never had. Hmm… at least I don't think he has any sprogs running around. Who knows these days, the way most people go around sowing their oats?"

"What? I can't believe you would say such a thing. So below the belt even Muhammad Ali would never punch that low."

"Sorry, I didn't really mean it, but you get my drift. People tend to…"

Bob raised a hand to stop her talking. "Don't go saying something you're likely to regret."

Sam chewed on the inside of her mouth. "All right. I'll stop there. I'm sure Rhys will talk when he feels able to deal with what's gone on. I'm prepared to wait. In the meantime…"

"In the meantime, you're going to milk the sympathy surrounding you and suck it up, right?"

"Piss off, Bob. I'm going to do nothing of the sort. The last thing I want is sympathy, dealing with that is a major issue. All I want is to crack on with the case we're working on and move on to the next one."

"What you need is to assess where your life is going to be in two, five, or even ten years' time. If you're not prepared to put the effort in now to achieve what lies ahead, then there's no hope for you."

Sam showed him the tip of her tongue. "Bollocks to you, too. I appreciate you mean well, but I know deep down that it would be a mistake for me to contact Rhys at this time.

Next week, next month, or next year, and it'll probably be a different ballgame."

"Whatever. All I can do is offer you advice from a bloke's perspective, it's up to you if you choose to ignore it."

"I am *not* ignoring it. I'm listening to my intuition and to my head, instead of what's in my heart."

"It's your prerogative."

"Indeed. Let's get back to the station. I have had enough of your lecturing to last me a lifetime."

"Hey, hang around, babe, I haven't even started yet. If two people are meant to be together, then nothing, earth, wind, or fire, should stand in their way. I believe that sums you and Rhys up perfectly. My old nan would say, 'You two need your heads knocking together to make you see sense.'"

Sam chuckled. "Funny, my gran used to say the same. I miss her dearly. She was a miserable bitch most of the time but she had her moments, usually when we were on our own together, where she showed true kindness and a different side to her personality."

"Mine was the same. I used to spend far more time with my gran than with my mother during my formative years. She died of cancer a few years ago. Tore my heart out, it did. Sad when a great influence leaves our lives."

"It is. Come on, the others will be wondering where we've got to with their lunch. Thanks for the chat, Bob."

"I've told you, anytime. We're all in this together. Life throws the weirdest shit at us when we're least expecting it. I genuinely believe it's to make us tougher."

"Maybe. Thanks anyway, for allowing me to bend your ear."

They reached the car and settled into their seats.

Sam put the radio on, but a call interrupted the music not long after. "DI Sam Cobbs. How may I help?"

"Sam, it's Alan. I might have something for you."

"Sounds intriguing. What's that?"

"I followed up with a family member—by the way, the mothers are on their way up to see you now, if they haven't already arrived. I think there was a delay in their departure. I digress. I spoke to Tara's sister. She let slip that one of Tara's ex-fellas has been poking around lately."

"Hmm... have you run a check on him? Is there anything on the system?"

"There was. He's been banged up for over a year."

"On what charge?"

"Burglary and assault."

Sam glanced at Bob who was looking thoughtful.

"Okay, that puts a different spin on things. Are you able to visit him?"

"I'm on my way over there now. Thought I'd bring you up to date during the journey."

"Thanks, Alan. Let me know how you get on, and we'll brace ourselves for the mothers' imminent arrival."

"Will do. Be in touch soon."

Sam ended the call and said, "Burglary and assault, that's a distinct possibility."

"Yeah, I suppose it depends if he's going to present a tight alibi or not."

"Exactly. In the meantime, we, or should I say, I, need to prepare for the victims' mothers showing up. Something I'm definitely not looking forward to."

THEY HADN'T BEEN BACK at the station long when Nick Travis rang her while she was going over yet more paperwork in her office. "Yes, Nick?"

"I have two ladies, a Mrs Knox and a Mrs Mansell, waiting in reception to see you, ma'am."

"I'll be right down. Is there a room free where I can speak with them?"

"I'll make sure the front office is available for you, unless you'd prefer to use one of the interview rooms?"

"No, the office will be more informal. See you shortly." Sam ended the call and opened her drawer. She withdrew a brush and ran it through her hair and touched up her makeup. Then she left the room and stopped off at Bob's desk. "They're here. I can handle it. You keep on top of things around here."

"Sure, not that there's a lot to keep on top of. Good luck."

"Thanks, I have a feeling your best wishes will be needed."

She took a leisurely walk down to the reception area, taking time to gather her thoughts.

The women, both dressed in black coats and shoes, were sitting in the reception area, staring at the wall ahead of them.

Sam approached. The woman in the seat closest to the door turned towards her. Sam gave the briefest of smiles. The woman nudged her companion.

"Hello, there. I'm DI Sam Cobbs."

"I'm Yvonne Knox, and this is Elizabeth Mansell."

"Liz," Mrs Mansell corrected her friend.

"Pleased to meet you, ladies. I've been expecting you." Sam swivelled to speak to the desk sergeant. "Is the room free, Sergeant?"

"It is, ma'am. Can I arrange for any drinks to be brought through to you?"

"Ladies?" Sam asked.

"Coffee, black, no sugar for me. What do you want, Liz?"

"White with one sugar for me, thank you."

"And I'll have coffee, white with one, thanks, Sergeant. Ladies, if you'd like to come with me?" Sam opened the door to the right of them, close to the main entrance, and entered the room. The sergeant had arranged three chairs around the rectangular table, two on one side and one on the other. Sam gestured for the ladies to take a seat and closed the door behind them.

"What can you tell us?" Yvonne asked on the way to her seat.

"Currently leads are thin on the ground. We've yet to receive the post-mortem results. Having those to hand usually gives us a better idea of what we're dealing with."

"Why the delay?" Liz asked.

"I'm guessing because of the state the bodies were in. Would I be right, Inspector?" Yvonne asked.

"As a nurse, you would appreciate what kind of damage we're talking about here. The pathologist wants to be sure he's got the right information to hand before he offers his expert opinion."

"What kind of information?" Liz was the first to ask.

"The actual cause of death. He'll be working closely with the Scenes of Crime Officers to try to obtain any evidence that wasn't destroyed in the fire. That's going to be the hard part in the process. I'm sure you don't need me to tell you how damaging a small fire can be, let alone one where a whole building is concerned. They're dealing with a complex crime scene, one that truly might take months to sift through, given the size of the cottage involved."

Liz gasped and clamped a hand over her mouth. She bowed her head, hiding the tears she was trying her hardest to hold back. Her hand dropped into her lap, and she mumbled, "Does that mean that we won't be able to lay them to rest yet?"

"Possibly. It's far too early to give you any information along those lines. I'm—" A knock on the door interrupted Sam. She shot out of her chair to open it.

The sergeant walked into the room carrying three mugs which he distributed before leaving again.

"Thanks, Nick, much appreciated."

Sam returned to her seat.

"You were saying?" Yvonne asked.

"Yes, that's right. I was about to say I'm going to have to ask you to bear with us during our enquiries."

"Easier said than done." Yvonne sat back and folded her arms, the seams on her coat straining.

"Honestly, I completely understand how frustrating all this waiting around for information must be for both of you. All I can assure you is that we're doing our very best to overcome the issues we're up against."

"Have you found anything out yet? Shouldn't you be out there now, searching for the killer?" Yvonne sat forward again and took a sip of her coffee.

"I promise you, we're doing what we can. CCTV footage has revealed that the Lexus wasn't being followed. I have an inspector in Coventry chasing up any background information that comes our way."

"Such as?"

"Actually, I've just received a call from him. When he spoke to Tara's sister, she told him that Tara's ex boyfriend had been hanging around lately. The detective is on his way around there now to interview him."

"Who is it?" Yvonne frowned and asked.

"I didn't get the name. I'm leaving Wareing to deal with things down in the Midlands. That's why the investigation is going slowly at this end, because your son and daughter weren't local. That's not to say our efforts are nominal, they're not, I assure you. But if a crime takes place in our area and the victims are local, it does make it a lot easier to chase up clues."

"So it was a waste of time us coming up here, is that what

you're saying?" Liz replied.

"Only time will tell. What I will ask you to do is to possibly manage your expectations because of the variables involved. This isn't me making excuses, I'm not in the habit of doing that, never have been. This is about the method in which the crime was committed."

"Are you telling us that it was planned?" Yvonne asked.

Sam shrugged. "It's looking more and more likely. The cottage was remote. Again, there were no witnesses in the vicinity, no close neighbours who we can rely on to provide the facts."

"This is terrible. All we want to know is how Tara and Daniel died, and here you are, telling us that you're unlikely to be able to fill in the blanks for weeks, maybe even months." Liz shook her head, and her chin dipped to her chest.

Yvonne reached for her friend's hand. "I'm sure it won't come to that, Liz. I have a good feeling about the inspector. I'm sure she won't let us down."

Sam smiled at the much-needed endorsement. "I won't, you have my word. Where are you ladies staying?"

"At the Wainwrights Hotel in town. We've made a provisional booking for a few days," Yvonne replied. "I suppose there's no point in asking if we can see our babies, is there?"

Sam swallowed down the bile that had materialised and batted away the image of the charred victims that had planted itself in her mind. "There would be no point. I'm sorry."

At that, both ladies broke down in tears. Leaving Sam feeling like a heartless bitch. The thing was, she also had a damning image of her own circulating her mind, that of Chris being pulled from the burning wreckage of his car.

What a diabolical end to a loved one's life, to go up in flames like that. It must be the most horrific sendoff known to man.

CHAPTER 5

"How long before we get there now?" Cathy asked eagerly.

The stunning views surrounding them had reignited a desire within to walk the hills and then laze around in the evening with her husband. They had both been working extra hours lately, a sign of the times with Covid tailing off and staff shortages on the rise.

"You're like a big kid. We'll get there when we get there."

Cathy pulled a face at him. "Spoilsport. I love this area so much. Maybe, just maybe, once the baby has grown up a little, perhaps we can toy with the idea of moving up here. What do you think?"

"Bloody hell, the baby hasn't even been born yet. Besides, have you truly considered the consequences of that statement? What the hell would our parents say? Us whisking their only grandchild away from Brighton? I'll tell you what they'd do, they'd absolutely go apeshit, and who could blame them? Even more devastating than that, what would we do about childcare? Your mum has offered to look after the baby for the first two years while you go back to work. How can we possibly turn that down with the cost of living going through the roof? It's not practical, love, sorry."

Cathy sighed and rested her head against the passenger window. "It was just a thought. Why does everything have to come down to money?"

Shelby laughed. "Because without it, we'd be up shit creek, and *everyone* else would be in the same boat with us. It's the way of the world. I can see people really taking stock in the future, more couples refusing to have children, due to the exorbitant costs involved in bringing them up."

She rubbed the slight bulge in her tummy. "Are you telling me you're regretting what lies ahead of us?"

"Did I say that? No, what I'm trying to get across is that we need to be cautious, to rein in our dreams and expectations in this life, chiefly because of the state the economy is in. Let's face it, neither of our businesses is exactly booming at present, is it?"

"True. I hate it when you talk sense. You've always been the more practical one out of the two of us."

Shelby reached for her hand and kissed the back of it. "We make a great team, always have and always will. Can't wait until there are three of us. There's no doubting there will be tough times ahead of us, but with our determination, we'll get through it all. Maybe we should put off any thoughts of moving to the area for a few years, minimum. We can make it a major ambition for our future."

"Okay, if you say so. Every time I visit this area, though, I have to say my whole existence changes. I know I'm probably talking shit and existence is more than likely the wrong word to use, blame my baby brain, but you know what I mean."

"I do. We unwind the second we hop over the border from Lancashire. The Lakes have always held a special place in my heart. Don't get me wrong, I'd jump at the chance of moving up here tomorrow, but my practical side tells me that

I would be living in a dream world to believe that was even on the cards. Then, of course, you've got the fact that property prices in this area are spinning out of control, yet another disastrous consequence of the pandemic."

Cathy sat upright and stared at him. "How do you know? You've been searching the internet already, haven't you?"

He smiled and raised an eyebrow. "I've told you before, our minds are always in sync. I'd love nothing more than upping sticks and having these phenomenal views on our doorstep. Let's just enjoy our time here, make the most of it and put aside our plans until a later date."

Cathy lifted his hand and kissed it the way he had kissed hers moments earlier. "Sounds like a great idea. Now… are we nearly there yet?"

He groaned. "Christ, I never thought our child would have a rival in the excitement stakes where holidays or days out were concerned."

"Charming. I'm eager to get unpacked and put my feet up, it's been a long week."

"It has, for both of us. Hey, can I remind you what time I get up every morning?"

"You don't need to. I'm always awake when you get out of bed at two anyway, I just pretend I'm still asleep otherwise you'll expect me to get up and make you a drink before you set off to work. No chance of that happening, hon, not in a month of Sundays."

"I knew it. Don't think I haven't caught you taking a sneaky peek at me now and again while I'm getting dressed."

They both laughed. The holiday spirit was definitely upon them. The stresses of running their own businesses set aside for the next week. This trip was all about them spending some quality, important time together before the baby came along in four months.

Cathy breathed out another contented sigh and leaned

her head against the window again as they wound their way through the country roads, the hills on either side of them acting like a comfort blanket during the rest of the journey.

She eventually dozed off until Shelby kissed her cheek.

"We're here," he whispered.

Sitting upright, Cathy took in her surroundings. "Damn, this is so beautiful. We couldn't ask for a better hideaway, could we?"

"I think that's the woman from the rental agency. They said it's their policy to send someone to meet us, show us how everything works, that sort of thing. Do you want to stay here or come on the guided tour with me?"

Cathy unfastened her seatbelt. "Try and stop me."

They left the vehicle and approached the smiling woman.

"Hi, I hope you've had a pleasant drive up here. I'm Annie. I'll leave you my number before I set off. You can contact me day or night if any problems arise during your stay."

"Hi, Annie. I'm Shelby, and this is Cathy. The journey wasn't too bad, got a bit congested on the roadworks coming up the M6. I bet everyone says the same. Anyway, we soon got through it. It's so kind of you to come out of your way to greet us. This is a beautiful area you live in."

"It is. Better during the summer when the days are longer, it gets dark far too early now. So glad you found the cottage while it was still light, it's a terrible job to find it in the dark. Most of our remote cottages are like that. Still, I'm sure that'll be an advantage to you, if you've come away for some peace and quiet."

"We have. Some alone time with each other. We decided to take an extra day off today. I thought it would take us around seven hours to get here. It wasn't far off that."

Annie smiled. "Not a drive I'd care to make. Still, it's better for you to travel up here at this time of year rather than tackle all the traffic in the summer months."

"My thoughts exactly. We can't wait to see inside. The vista here is amazing."

"Glad you like it. Let me show you around. It's a quaint cottage, one of our more popular rentals. I must warn you, it's in need of a little updating here and there. Nothing to deter you from having a good time, though. The owners are planning to withdraw the property over the winter to spruce it up a bit, ready for the next season."

"We'll bear that in mind. The photos on your website didn't trigger any warning bells for me, so I'm sure it'll be fine just as it is. But we appreciate your honesty."

Annie smiled and walked ahead of them. She unlocked the door and handed Shelby the key. "I'll show you the downstairs first. We've put the welcome pack you ordered on the kitchen table. I took the liberty of placing the milk and cheese in the fridge."

"Very thoughtful of you, thanks," Cathy replied. "This is such a sweet place. Small but adequate for our purposes. There's only the two of us, there's ample room for us to spread our wings if necessary. Is it a gas or electric hob? Not that I'm planning on doing much cooking while we're here."

"Electric. It depends on what you're used to. Easy enough to use, though."

"I'm gas at home. It'll give me an excuse not to cook anything. Shelby can do his own fry-ups in the morning."

Shelby snorted. "Nothing new there. That's the door leading to the garden, is it?"

Locating the key on the worktop, Annie inserted it into the back door and opened it to show them the small, pretty garden with its splendid view of the mountains beyond. "It's much better during the day, obviously. There are a couple of sun loungers in the garden shed at the bottom, feel free to use them whilst you're here."

Cathy nodded. "I hope we get some sun during the week, but the forecast is telling us otherwise."

"Oops, yes, sorry. I have a habit of telling people and sometimes forget what time of year it is. No sign of an Indian summer this year," Annie replied.

"Unfortunately," Cathy grumbled. "I could have done with topping up my tan ready for the winter."

Shelby stepped back towards the door. "Is the lounge in here?"

Annie locked the back door and removed the key. She placed it back on the worktop and rushed past Cathy to catch up with Shelby. "Yes. There's a comfy sofa and armchairs. Here, in the cupboard," Annie opened one of the doors to a large sideboard sitting along one of the walls, "there are several board games. A pack of cards et cetera. Just have a snoop around. There are a few DVDs here, in case you want to watch a film. You have Sky TV on hand, so that should keep you entertained as well, if you need it."

"We're not really ones to while away our time watching TV all day. My wife prefers to read, and I play poker online most days," Shelby replied.

"Blimey. For money?" Annie asked.

"Of course. I only set a small budget each day but I have to say I'm quite lucky, or I have been up until now. Only been doing it for a few months."

"Against my better judgement," Cathy chipped in. "Although I can't complain about the results. You can see why people get addicted and end up with massive debts hanging over their heads after getting involved with these sites."

"That was going to be my next question, about the addiction side of things. Not that I've ever tried anything as… adventurous as poker before."

Shelby hitched up a shoulder. "That's why I set a daily

limit. So far this month I'm in profit. I'll keep going until that profit disperses. I know when to call a halt to things without dipping into my savings. Cathy wouldn't allow it anyway."

"Too right. He's trying to cobble enough money together to decorate the nursery."

Annie glanced down at Cathy's tummy. "You're pregnant?"

Cathy blushed and nodded. "Yes, I'm not showing much right now, but we're excited about what's to come. This week's holiday is about celebrating our new arrival, maybe taking a break while we have the energy and can afford it before the little one arrives in the spring."

"How wonderful. Well, I hope the holiday is a memorable one for you and the rest of the pregnancy goes well. Maybe I should sort out a bucket for you and place it beside your bed, just in case." Annie laughed.

"Now there's an excellent thought," Shelby said.

Cathy playfully gave him a punch in the arm. "I'm not that bad… yet. Seriously, I haven't had any trouble with morning sickness. My friend has suffered terribly. She has to sit in the loo for hours first thing in the morning."

"Poor thing. I've never had children, I can imagine that would be traumatic to deal with. Right, shall I show you upstairs?"

"Yes, please. Can't wait to wake up and see the views in the morning from the bedroom. I take it they're as good up there?" Cathy asked.

"You'll see for yourself in the morning. Come with me." Annie ran through a few extra things they might need to know during the trip up the staircase. "The recycling bins are collected on Thursday here. They're pretty much the same all over the country now, I should imagine. Just put the bin in the lane outside, if you wouldn't mind. The nearest shop is about half a mile away. It's a small general store. If you're looking for a supermarket, the nearest one would be in Workington, around fifteen minutes away. Not too bad."

"Great news. Thanks for that. And the nearest pub?" Shelby asked.

"Just up the road. You might have passed it, unless you came from the other way. It's called the White Horse. They do really good value-for-money bar meals. That'll give you more money to spend on a poker game."

"Please, don't give him any ideas," Cathy shouted from the back.

"Here we are. This is the smaller of the two bedrooms. The bed is made up for you, just in case."

"In case we fall out over your gambling, so think on," Cathy warned Shelby and wagged a finger at him.

"Duly noted, dearest wifey. Is the main bedroom next door?" Shelby asked from the doorway, taking a step backwards.

"Yes, if you'd like to lead the way," Annie said.

The three of them walked into the tired-looking bedroom, with its 1980s floral frieze border plastered haphazardly around the top of the room. There was a satin throw on the bed in a ghastly cerise pink that reminded Cathy of her grandmother's bed. She shuddered, reflecting how her gran had died in that very bed, with her family all around her.

"Are you cold, love?" Shelby flung an arm around her shoulder.

"No. I'll tell you later. This is nice." She walked towards the window, and disappointment struck with the lack of light left to take in the views.

"Not a good view?" Annie asked. "It'll be better in the morning. Right, that's all I have to show you. Do you have any questions you wish to ask before I leave?"

Cathy and Shelby glanced at each other.

"I think you've covered pretty much everything," Shelby replied.

The three of them went back downstairs, and Annie left the cottage.

Cathy went through to the lounge and threw herself onto the sofa. "I'm cream-crackered. I'm not moving for at least half an hour."

Shelby swooped down and gave her a kiss. "You stay where you are, I'll ferry the bags in. First, I'll pop the kettle on."

"It probably won't suit you." Cathy grinned. "Now you're making me feel guilty."

"Don't, I know how much travelling takes out of you. Stay there. Want me to find something on TV for you to watch?"

"Nope. I'll just sit here, resting my eyes for a moment or two."

"You do that." Her husband closed the door on his way out.

Cathy drifted off to sleep within seconds. The next thing she knew, Shelby was waking her up with a nice mug of tea.

"Here you go. I even found you a shortbread biscuit to satisfy your hunger pangs until we can get to the pub. Fancy going out this evening?"

"That would be lovely. I think I need to freshen up first. We forgot to check if there's any hot water."

"There is. I've already sussed it out, there's a combi boiler here. We're on oil heating, and the shower is electric."

"You have been busy. Please tell me you've unpacked all the bags and put the clothes away as well."

Shelby tutted. "Now don't go taking the piss."

She slapped a hand over her chest. "Me? I wouldn't dream of it. I'll take my drink upstairs, unpack, and then jump in the bath."

"I could always join you."

"Not if we intend going out this evening."

"You win. Once I'm in bed tonight, I won't want to get out again."

"That's settled then. See you soon. No doubt you'll be busy once my back is turned. I hope you win enough to pay for dinner."

He beamed at her, and she trotted up the stairs to the main bedroom, where she spent the next twenty minutes putting all their clothes into the chest of drawers and wardrobes, although she did hesitate for a few minutes, wondering if she was doing the right thing or not after the mustiness of the old furniture hit her full in the face.

Ugh... I hope the owners have the good sense to renew the furniture when they get around to sprucing up the place. I think it's long overdue.

She scanned the room and saw a spray bottle of room freshener sitting on the flaking windowsill. She squirted it around the room, more than she would normally dare to do at home, and the mustiness receded, not much, but it would be enough for them to get a decent night's sleep, she hoped.

Job done, Cathy took her towel into the bathroom and groaned at the black mould she spotted in the corner of the tiles surrounding the bath. "Bang goes my relaxing half an hour in the tub. I'll have a damn shower instead." She turned to inspect the shower and cringed. The grout in the tiles, especially on the wall closest to the showerhead, had patches of mould along the bottom edge and all the way up where the two sections joined. "How can anyone even consider renting this place out in this state? I wish I'd noticed it before that Annie had left."

"Who are you talking to?" Shelby called up the stairs.

"Sorry, just having a conversation with the baby." She sniggered. *Well, it was better than telling him the truth, he'll think I'm a bloody nutter.*

After undressing, she ran the hot water and then dived under it before it had a chance to run cold on her. She completed the shower in record speed, fearing she might come out dirtier than when she stepped into the damn thing.

Gross. I can't put up with that all week. I'll have to work on Shelby over dinner, see if he'll ring the agency in the morning to do a swap. It's disgusting to expect people to pay top dollar for a shit-hole like this. Why hadn't I noticed it before?

Cathy dried herself off in the bedroom.

Shelby arrived moments later and hugged her tightly. "Glad we came? It's a fabulous place, isn't it? Nice and cosy."

Cathy smiled up at him and nodded. How could she reveal her true feelings now? "We need to get out and explore tomorrow. I don't want to be stuck inside all the time whilst we are here."

He pulled his head back and frowned. "I thought that was the idea for us coming here? Chilling out, spending time alone before the baby arrives?"

"It was. It is. But after getting a glimpse of the views, what there was for us to see, I thought sod it, we must make the most of our time here. Who knows when we'll be able to climb the hills and go sightseeing around all the wonderful places on our doorstep in the near future with a little hooman to care for twenty-four-seven?"

"I wholeheartedly agree. Let's finish getting ready and get out of here. I'm starving, haven't had anything since breakfast."

"I did warn you not to skip lunch."

"I should have listened." He pecked her on the nose and then released her. "Fifteen minutes tops, and then we leave, okay?"

"I'll be ready, don't worry about me."

. . .

THE EVENING WAS DARKER than they had anticipated, if that was possible. Shelby had to guide their path to the car with the torch on his phone. "Sod this, not having any streetlights to aid our trip. How ridiculous."

Cathy laughed. "Ah, the beauty of living in a remote location. I'm sure it would appeal to some full-time. Sadly, not us. Don't let it spoil our holiday."

"No intentions of it doing that, I'm just being a typical Brit on holiday. I always have to find something to complain about."

I could think about a few things to add to the list but I won't bother!

The pub was a typical rural gathering place for the locals. They were scrutinised by every customer sitting in the bar the moment they set foot through the front door. Cathy cringed and clung to Shelby's arm. He left her at a table and placed an order for drinks at the bar. She glanced around her, uncomfortable under the regulars' gazes. In the end, she focussed on the open fire over to the right, instead.

"Here you go. I bet you were dying for a nice glass of red, weren't you?"

"Orange juice will have to do for the foreseeable. Did you get a menu?"

"I asked. It's all on the specials board behind the bar."

"Not sure I can see that far."

Shelby ended up reading out the choices on offer, and they both decided to go for the lasagne and chips.

"I'd love a steak but fancied a sirloin, I'm not really into rump. I'll pick up some at the supermarket tomorrow. We could have a romantic dinner for two, how about that?" he asked.

Cathy sipped at her juice and gathered his hand in hers. "Sounds perfect to me."

Thankfully, the service was excellent and the meal arrived

within ten minutes. The locals soon lost interest in them, which was a relief, allowing them to enjoy their meals without feeling like it was feeding time at the zoo.

"Annie was right, the food here is fantastic," Shelby said. He put the last forkful of lasagne into his mouth and pushed the plate away. "I'm stuffed."

"I was hoping you'd help me with mine. I can't manage another mouthful." Cathy stared at her half-eaten lasagne and slid her plate towards him.

"Not a chance in hell, love. Sorry. You're going to have to leave it."

"Bugger, and risk the barman giving me the evil eye for daring to leave any?"

Shelby laughed. "As if. We've paid for it, why should it matter if you leave it or not?"

Placing down her knife and fork, she admitted defeat and stacked her plate on top of her husband's. "It was delicious, but the portion size would need to be cut in half if I thought about having it again."

"What are you insinuating, that I'm a pig?"

She looked sideways at him and shrugged. "If the cap fits."

"Bloody cheek. I take it dessert is off the menu then?"

"You can have that when we get home."

"What are we waiting for?"

They said farewell to the barman, and Cathy smiled at the locals who smiled back at her on the way out.

"See you again soon," a wizened old man sitting at the bar called after them.

Shelby waved and responded, "That you will. The food was excellent."

They got in the car.

"The locals soon came around. A bit stiff to begin with, eh?" Shelby said.

Cathy nodded. "The atmosphere was a tad prickly at first.

Makes you wonder what it's like for the locals, you know, being inundated with tourists throughout the year. The village probably never feels like their own."

"I hadn't thought about it. I suppose you're right. The upside to living in a small community like this is that the money we choose to spend here doubtless helps maintain the community, keeps it going if you like."

"If you think so." Weary beyond words, Cathy's head hit the window. She couldn't wait to get back home and into bed. "I think I'm going to sleep for forty-eight hours solid, if that's all right with you?"

"We'll see."

They drove back to the cottage that was lit up in their main beam ahead of them.

"I hate that it's so dark around here," Cathy grumbled.

"I suppose you'd get used to it after a while. Don't let it spoil our stay, hon."

Cathy entered the cottage ahead of Shelby, and when he went to close the front door, something slotted into the opening to prevent him. "What the fuck is going on here?"

Suddenly, the door burst open and a masked figure blocked the doorway. The person held a long-bladed knife in their right hand. "Get back," the electronic voice ordered.

Shelby scrambled backwards and knocked into his wife who was standing there, dumbstruck. He gripped her hands in his. "Please, what do you want from us? We're here on holiday, we don't carry much cash, if that's what you're after."

"I'm not. In the lounge. Now."

Cathy stared at her husband, words failing her as her pulse rate escalated. She tried to address the situation for the sake of the baby, but when she discreetly placed her fingers over several pulse points on her neck and her wrist, she realised how miserably she had failed. "Shelby, we have to do something," she whispered in his ear.

"Like what?" he replied out of the corner of his mouth.

"Shut up! You speak when I tell you to. Sit in the armchairs, opposite each other."

"I'll have to move one of them," Shelby said.

"Do it then, moron, don't make this into a drama."

Shelby settled Cathy into one of the armchairs and moved the other one into place so that their knees were virtually touching.

"Too close. Shift it back a bit."

Shelby carried out the instructions whilst staring at Cathy. "It's going to be all right," he mouthed.

She doubted if that was true.

The intruder dropped the holdall they were carrying on the floor beside Shelby. It clattered noisily. She shuddered as dark images filled her mind.

"Keep calm," Shelby mouthed.

"Shut up. I won't allow you to communicate." The intruder unzipped the bag and removed several tools: a hammer, a hacksaw, a set of pliers and a small blowtorch.

Cathy's gaze shot between the implements and then back to her husband. *Please, no, this can't be happening! Not to us. Please, God, protect us in our hour of need. Strike this person down before they can cause us any harm.*

"Cathy," the intruder said, shocking her. "I want you to pick up the hammer and use it on your husband."

Shocked, Cathy stared at the masked person and vigorously shook her head. "No. I can't. I won't. You can't force me to do it."

"Cathy, do as you're told," Shelby pleaded.

"No. I won't," Cathy repeated, her heart rate thundering in her ears.

"It's okay. I'll forgive you if you hurt me," Shelby assured her, his eyes damp with tears.

"There will be nothing to forgive because I'm not doing it," she said adamantly.

Her husband closed his eyes and shook his head. When he opened them again, Cathy was in tears. "Do it, Cathy."

"I can't, Shel. Don't make me. I would never hurt you, my love."

The intruder laughed and applauded her brave words. "What a star she is. Most women would relish the chance to give their husbands a good hiding. Oh well, the choice was hers. Now it's down to you, *Shel.*"

Shelby's head jerked, and he shouted, "What the fuck are you talking about? Why don't you leave us alone? Are you getting off on us being terrified?"

"I might be. Pick up the hammer and strike your wife's hand."

Shelby hesitated, forcing the intruder to pick up the hammer and place it in Shelby's trembling hand.

"Do it. This request comes with a warning: if you don't carry out my instructions to the letter, I'll have little option but to kill her and your unborn baby."

Shelby's face wrinkled. Cathy could tell he was in turmoil.

"I'm sorry, Cathy. Please forgive me for what I'm about to do."

Cathy's eyes widened as he raised the hammer above his head. She squeezed her eyes shut, waiting for the impact, but it never came. Her eyes flew open again to find her husband wrestling with the intruder, calling the masked person all the names under the sun.

"No, Shelby, don't do this. Stop. I don't want us to die."

The intruder dodged the blows Shelby was aiming with the hammer and jabbed intermittently at Shelby's midsection with the knife.

"No... please, stop this, think of the baby," Cathy screamed.

Shelby paused to look at Cathy. While he was distracted, the intruder pounced on the opportunity and plunged the knife into Shelby's side. He stared at Cathy for a few frantic moments, the wind knocked out of him, until he glanced down to see the blood oozing from the wound.

"I warned you. You should have done things my way. Now things have escalated, there's no going back. Shelby, before you die, I want you to know that your wife and child won't be far behind you. You're a very foolish couple. You deserve to go out together."

Cathy screamed, loud enough for the glass lamp in the corner of the room to vibrate on the side table. "No, Shelby. You can't leave me. I won't allow you to leave like this," she yelled. She got to her feet and ran at the intruder. "You bastard. How dare y—?"

Her sentence was cut short when the knife pierced her stomach. She didn't care about her life, only about that of her baby. The blade twisted, deeper and deeper. Cathy groaned, stumbled backwards and collapsed into her seat again. She stared, her eyes fully open, at her husband. His face had paled, and his eyelids were drooping. She reached out a hand. The intruder slapped it down again with the handle of the knife, shocking her.

Cathy turned her head towards the masked person and she asked one question, "Why?"

The masked face came closer. Their gazes latched, the intruder said, "Because I can. Happiness is the root of all evil. No one has a right to be happy in this life... no one."

"What? I don't understand what you're talking about. Why us?"

"I saw you. It's obvious how much you love and adore one

another. That's not right. No one has the right to be totally dependent on another person the way you are."

"That doesn't make sense," Cathy said, her breath faltering along with her pulse. Once erratic, now it had significantly slowed down. "Shelby, stay awake. You dare give up on me. I love you, you hear me… don't give u…" Cathy's words died in her throat when Shelby's head dropped to one side. "Shelby… don't leave me. We can get through this."

The intruder laughed and placed a finger on Shelby's neck. "It's a waste of time… he's dead. Gone but not forgotten, eh?"

The tears cascaded down Cathy's face. What was the point in fighting or pleading for her life now? Now that her loving husband was dead? What was the point of her going on? She knew in her heart that the wound she was carrying had already ended their baby's life. *Why? What's the point in going on without them?* "Finish me off, you might as well. I have nothing left now that they're both dead."

"Come now, I expected better of you. Where's that fighting spirit gone?" the intruder taunted.

"I have no fight left in me. I'm fading fast."

The intruder rooted through Cathy's pockets and brought out her phone. "I'll give you the chance to make a final call."

Her mood switched at the prospect of calling for help. "Who can I call?"

"The choice is yours. Make it count. My guess is you'll be dead within ten minutes, if not sooner."

Cathy held out her hand, and the intruder placed her mobile in her palm. She studied it, hoping it would give her the courage to dial a number, but which one should she choose? Her hand shook. Finger poised, she searched the bottom of the keypad and tapped her finger on the nine three times.

"Hello, emergency services, how can I help?"

"Please, hurry, I need help. My husband and baby are dead…"

"Okay, calm down. Can you tell me where you are?"

"No. we're on… holiday…" Her breath caught in her throat. Cathy struggled to say anything else, her mind was shutting down, her consciousness slipping. She could hear the woman on the other end of the line talking but could no longer hold a conversation with her.

The intruder checked her pulse and removed the phone from her feeble grip.

"Hello, can you hear me?" the operator shouted.

"No, she can't. She's dead," the intruder confirmed and disconnected the call.

With them both dead, there was only one thing left to do, tamper with the evidence, concealing what had taken place at the crime scene.

Out came a small can of petrol, the contents of which were poured over the two chairs where the bodies lay. A box of matches soon followed. The intruder moved towards the door, struck the match and aimed it at the chair where Shelby lay dead. Another match was thrown. It landed in Cathy's lap. The intruder left the cottage, ran back up the lane towards the main road and jumped into the waiting vehicle.

CHAPTER 6

Sam was enjoying a deep, restful sleep for a change. At the trilling of the phone, she sat upright and switched on the light. Sonny raised his head to look at her and then flopped again. It was just past midnight.

"Go back to sleep, boy."

Her eyes took a while to adjust. She glanced at the tiny screen and saw Des's name which forced her to answer it. "Hey, what's up?"

"I've got another one, Sam. You'd better get out here right away."

"Another arson attack?"

"Yep. Two dead. Luckily, a neighbour spotted the fire and called the brigade. They arrived within a few minutes to extinguish the fire, after attending another call nearby, however, it was too late for the victims."

"Oh shit! Give me your location, and I'll get dressed and come over."

"Ugh… sorry to disturb you this early, Sam."

"It doesn't matter. The address?" *It's not like I'm busy, is it? Who needs a good night's sleep anyway?*

She jotted down the details he gave her and hung up. "Geez, what am I going to do with you? I can't wake Doreen up at this time, she'd string me up. I'll take you with me, just this once. Don't go getting used to it, you hear me?"

Sonny tilted his head one way and then the other. She ran into the bathroom, flung some cold water over her rosy cheeks and quickly gave her teeth a brush, aware that she'd eaten garlic bread and very little else for dinner. It was supposed to be her weekend off, so she'd thought it would be worth the risk. Des was bound to rib her about the stench when she got to the scene.

Sam flew down the stairs, grabbed a bottle of water out of the fridge, attached Sonny's leash and bundled her dog into the back seat of her car. "Sorry, no time for a wee for either of us. I'll sort you out when we get there, how's that?"

Sonny whimpered and lay down, resting his head on his front paws. Sam drove towards the scene, thankful that the village of Camerton was only ten minutes from where she lived. When she arrived, she found the rural lane lit by temporary floodlights. Sam ruffled Sonny's head, assured him she wouldn't be long and donned a paper suit. The cottage had been cordoned off. The damage wasn't too bad, not when compared to the first fire, but bad enough for Des to make a connection and to insist on her attendance at the scene.

After signing the Crime Scene Log and putting booties on, she entered the cottage. "Des, it's Sam, are you around?"

"Through here, in the lounge. Keep coming." Des was giving a few members of his team instructions and sent them on their way when he'd finished. The lounge was black, no smoke left in the room, nevertheless, the smell was noticeable all the same. She approached Des who was now crouching, examining the first of the bodies.

"They were killed before the fire was started, is that why you called me?" Sam asked.

Des wore a strange expression. "Jesus, what in God's name is that smell?"

"Umm... it's my weekend off. I indulged in a little more garlic bread than I probably should have. I make no apologies... I repeat, it's supposed to be my weekend off."

"Can't stand the stuff myself. If you're doing your best to keep prospective partners away, then I'd say you've succeeded."

Sam shook her head and kept quiet.

When the awkward silence descended, he turned to look up at her. "I'm sorry, that was bang out of order, too near the knuckle, wasn't it? My big mouth strikes again."

"Whatever. Don't push me, Des. Just give me the facts, and I'll be out of your hair soon enough."

"Ever the professional. I apologise again, Sam."

Her stare intensified, upping his discomfort. "The victims? How did they die?" As tempting as it was, she refrained from tapping her foot and folding her arms.

"Preliminary examinations are telling me they were both stabbed."

"Did they bleed out or were they still alive when the fire was started?"

"The PM will reveal anything else I need to confirm the COD."

She nodded and scanned the room. "The chairs were placed so they were facing each other, I wonder why."

"Perhaps to force one victim to watch as the other was attacked and killed."

"Hmm... maybe." Her eyes narrowed. "What if they were forced to hurt each other? Could they have possibly inflicted the wounds themselves while the killer, or should I say perpetrator, watched?"

It took a while for Des to reply. He stood and shook out his legs. "Anything is possible."

"That's my theory and I'm sticking to it until you supply information to counter it. Just the two of them here? I wonder if this is a holiday cottage, again."

"I'm surmising that's the case, what with the location and how tired the upstairs looks. Hard to tell what the downstairs was like, the fire damage is more noticeable down here, obviously."

"How come the house isn't a total mess?"

"The neighbour called it in before the fire had a chance to catch hold properly."

Sam remained thoughtful. "I didn't see any neighbouring houses on my way here."

"Correct, there weren't any. The woman lives further down the road, just around the corner. She happened to be out walking her dog."

"Ah, I see. Have you sent her packing?"

"No, I asked her to return home and told her that a *professional* officer would call in to get the facts from her this evening or they might leave it until tomorrow."

Sam grinned sarcastically. "I'll stop by and see her before I leave, if she's still up. Anything else you can give me at this stage?"

"Not really. I'll be conducting the post-mortems later today, if you fancy joining me."

She screwed up her nose. "I think I'll give it a miss, if it's all the same to you."

"Your choice. Always prefer to ask, never one to insist, you know that."

"I'm going to track down the witness. I'll call back to see you before I leave."

"I'll probably be here for hours. Good luck."

Sam smiled and left the charred cottage. She stripped off

her suit and shoe covers and deposited them in the evidence bag at the front door. After pausing to take in her surroundings for a second or two, she trotted back to the car and received an enthusiastic welcome from Sonny. "Now calm down, you. I have to make one more stop, and then we'll head home, I promise."

Sonny resumed his chilled-out position. Sam started the engine and continued the drive down the lane. Just around the corner, the neighbouring property came into view. *Hmm... so not quite as isolated as the first property. Was the killer aware of that fact?*

Sonny sat up when she pulled up outside the cottage. "Stay there, boy. I won't be too long." She lowered the two back windows three inches to ensure a good airflow, something she should have thought about earlier, on the way to the scene. A light was on in the front downstairs room. She pushed open the gate. The door opened ahead of her during her walk up the path.

"Hello there. I'm DI Sam Cobbs."

"I was told to expect someone. Come in, I'm Janet Blower. I live here alone, except for my dog, Tyson."

Sam produced her ID, and the woman studied it with the assistance of the porch light.

"Tyson? Is it a large dog?" Sam asked. She hadn't noticed any barking at her untimely presence.

"No. It was my son's idea. He's a cutie, a French bulldog, he's in the front room. Quiet as a mouse usually."

"I have a cockapoo. I had to bring him with me this evening. I received the call while I was off duty."

"Would you like to bring him in? I don't mind, and Tyson gets on well with other dogs."

"He's fine. I shouldn't keep you too long."

"The offer still stands. Come this way." Mrs Blower

showed her through to the room at the front, overlooking the road.

"Here he is, all tucked up in his bed next to the fire. I didn't fancy going back to bed, so I switched it on earlier."

Sam smiled. The cute dog was a fawn colour, and his ears pricked up when they entered the room, but he didn't move a muscle. "He's a sweetheart. I have to laugh at his name, though."

"I know. My son has a wicked sense of humour. Anyway, you're not here to discuss our pets. How can I help? Were there people inside the house at the time of the fire?"

Sam cringed. She had assumed that someone would have told Mrs Blower about the victims, either Des or the fire brigade. "Sorry to have to tell you this, but yes, there were two victims involved. A man and a woman."

Mrs Blower shook her head, clearly upset by the news. "I was hoping they would have been out when the fire started. Luckily, I saw a small blaze out of the corner of my eye last night as I passed the cottage. Tyson was busy pulling me up the lane instead of going in the opposite direction, which he usually does in the evening. It's as if he had a sixth sense that there was something going on up there."

"They can be very intuitive at times. That's why they make perfect service and search and find dogs. I have to ask, did you see anyone near the cottage, or was it too dark out there?"

"I always take a torch with me at night. I had it shining on the lane and I thought I saw someone up ahead of me. Tyson made a huffing sound, he rarely barks. I thought it must have been a fox or something along those lines. Do you think someone was responsible for the fire?"

"It looks that way." Sam gulped and then relayed the piece of news that would rock the woman's world. "Unfortunately, both the victims were found dead in the lounge. They had wounds that possibly indicate they were murdered."

Mrs Blower slapped her hands over her cheeks. "My God. How? Why? So I might have seen the person who killed them leaving the property?"

"I think that's a distinct possibility."

"Oh my. I don't know what to say. Is it normal for one's pulse to race in these circumstances? I feel terrible."

Sam shot across the room, knelt beside Mrs Blower and felt her pulse. Sweat poured from the woman's brow. "Do you have any medical issues?"

"High blood pressure. I've never had to deal with anything like this before."

"I'm going to call an ambulance." Sam removed her phone from her pocket and dialled nine-nine-nine. "What's the name of the cottage?"

"Primrose Cottage, Drayton Lane."

Sam smiled and patted the woman's hand. "Try to remain calm. I'm sure it's nothing to worry about, it's me being cautious, that's all."

"My heart is racing, I'm having trouble catching my breath. Please, I'm scared. Tell them to hurry."

"Hello, this is DI Cobbs. I'm with a lady at Primrose Cottage, Drayton Lane, Camerton. Can you send an ambulance ASAP, please?"

"One is on the way now," the woman on control said. "What's wrong, can you tell me?"

"Yes, racing heart rate, pulse is sky high, and she's breaking out in a sweat. How long before the ambulance gets here?"

"They're on the way. Should be there within ten to fifteen minutes, twenty at the most. I'll stay on the line until they arrive. Can you loosen her clothes if they are tight around her neck and chest?"

"I'm doing it now. I've never had to deal with this type of thing before. Is she going to be all right?"

"I'm sure we'll get her through this together. Try to keep calm at all times. Make sure the patient remains conscious, that's vitally important. How is she doing?"

"How are you, Mrs Blower?" Sam asked.

"It's Janet," she replied breathlessly.

Sam tugged at the clothing around the woman's neck, again. "You're doing well, this will make you more comfortable."

Tyson got out of his basket and sniffed Sam's leg. She petted him, and he jumped up at Janet.

"He's so sensitive. I'm all right, lovey. Now be a good boy and go back to your bed."

"The lady sounds perky enough," the woman on control noted.

"Maybe it's just me who is panicking, but I'd much rather err on the side of caution than ignore the signs."

"Quite right, too," the operator confirmed. "Can you feel her pulse for me? Is there any significant change there?"

Sam felt Janet's wrist again and found it difficult to determine if there was any change or not. "I'm sorry, I'm not sure."

"Don't worry. What about her colour, has that altered in the slightest?"

"Still the same. If anything, I don't think she is sweating quite so much."

"That's excellent news. I'm in touch with the crew, they're five minutes away from you now. Is the cottage easy to find?"

"Not too bad. I was next door at a crime scene, there are a few forensic vehicles outside that property. Tell them to drive past the first cottage and Primrose is just around the next bend."

The operator relayed the information to the paramedics then came back on the line and spoke to Sam once more.

"Okay, they should be with you shortly. Dare I ask what sort of crime scene you were attending?"

"A fire with two victims."

The operator tutted. "I think my colleague dealt with the call earlier this evening."

"It was Mrs Blower, sorry, Janet, who rang nine-nine-nine. I was interviewing her about the incident when she took a turn for the worse."

"Ah, that makes sense. It's probably the shock kicking in. We'll keep a close eye on her until the paramedics get there."

Sam smiled at Janet. "How are you feeling now?"

"About the same, dear. I'm so sorry to be causing you all this trouble, you have enough on your plate as it is, without having to deal with a foolish old woman like me."

"Don't you even think that, Janet. No one could have anticipated you taking a turn like this. The interview can wait, your health is far more important."

"I agree," the operator chipped in. "Not long to wait now, they're just outside the village."

Sam strained an ear, hoping to pick up the siren. Nothing yet.

Another few stressful moments passed before finally, Sam could make out the siren. "I can hear them now. I'll go and open the door for them and leave it ajar. The lady has a small dog, it's not aggressive, though."

"Okay, I'll end the call as soon as they're with you. Well done for keeping calm throughout."

"It was a joint effort." Sam patted Janet's hand again. "Are you feeling any better now?"

"I don't think so. I should call my son, Richard. He needs to know."

Janet pointed to her phone on the coffee table next to Sam. She reached for it and handed it to Janet.

"If you can pull up his number, I'll place the call."

Janet's hand shook. She punched in the passcode and groaned. "Damn thing. Fat fingers. Here you go, that's him. I hope we don't wake him."

"Don't worry, as soon as the paramedics arrive, I'll make the call." The siren's wail ceased when the ambulance drew up outside. "I won't be long, I forgot to open the door."

Sam greeted the paramedics and ushered them into the lounge. "This is Janet Blower."

The older of the two male paramedics got down on one knee beside Janet and carried out an examination. Sam left them to it and stepped into the hallway to call Janet's son.

The phone rang and rang. Sam glanced at her watch; it was just after one-thirty in the morning. She cringed when a groggy voice answered.

"Mum, what the hell do you want, ringing at this time of the morning?"

"Richard. This is DI Sam Cobbs. I'm with your mother now. Please, there's no need for you to be alarmed. She's in safe hands."

"Shit! What's wrong with her?" Richard sounded instantly more alert, on the edge of panic.

"The paramedics are assessing her now, I'd rather not speculate. She asked me to call you. I think they'll be admitting her to hospital."

"What for? You're not making sense."

"She has a racing pulse and is sweating profusely, that's all I can tell you for now."

"I'll get dressed. Where are they going to take her?"

"Let me ask." Sam knocked on the lounge door and entered. "I have Janet's son on the line. Can you tell me anything more?"

"We suspect it's a mild heart attack."

"And will you be taking her to hospital?" Sam asked.

"Yes, she'll be going to Whitehaven. He can join us there

at Accident and Emergency."

"Thanks. I'll pass it on." She closed the door again so that Janet couldn't overhear the conversation. "They're taking her to Whitehaven A and E with a suspected heart attack."

"Oh fuck! Shit, sorry about my language. I'll get there as soon as I can."

"Drive safely, there's no need to rush. I've been with her for around twenty minutes. She doesn't seem to be in any immediate danger."

"Thanks, we'll be there soon. Was she at home?"

"Yes. I was attending a nearby incident and called in to see her for a witness statement."

"Witness statement for what?"

"An incident which took place next door. A blaze broke out, and your mother called the fire brigade."

"And the shock brought this on? Is that what you're saying? Forgive me if I've misunderstood, I've only just woken up."

"Possibly. I would rather leave the speculation to the doctors at the hospital."

"Of course. Thank you for informing me. Send her our love. We'll get dressed and be at the hospital within twenty minutes."

"I'll pass on the message." This time, Sam ended the call before Richard could badger her with another bout of questions. She dipped back into the lounge. "How's it going?"

Janet seemed far more settled and relaxed than she had been with Sam before the paramedics had arrived, leading her to believe they had given her some form of medication to relieve her stress and the turmoil her body was possibly going through.

"We're ready to rock and roll. You're feeling a bit better, aren't you, Janet?"

"I am. Thanks to all of you. I don't mind telling you, I

thought I was a goner there."

Sam winked and squeezed Janet's shoulder. "I can tell that you're a born fighter. The docs will soon have you up and running around the ward."

Janet's smile slipped. "What will happen to Tyson? If Richard is coming to be with me at the hospital, who will look after him for me?"

Sam grinned. "If you'll allow me to, I can take him overnight and make arrangements to drop him off to Richard in the morning, how's that?"

"What? You don't even know me. I can't believe you'd do that for me."

"I'm a dog lover. The dogs come first, don't they?"

"You're too kind. I'd appreciate that so much, dear. You're an absolute treasure."

"Hopefully, you'll be back here before you know it. One less thing for you to stress over, isn't it? He'll be fine, Sonny gets on great with other dogs." Her heart dropped at the thought of Sonny playing with Benji, running free and without restraints at the park.

"Are you all right?" the younger paramedic asked.

"Sorry, deep in thought. A friend recently lost their dog, he was Sonny's playmate at the park."

"Right, we're going to have to make a move, get this young lady settled in a hospital bed for the night," the older paramedic said.

"One quick question, if I may? Janet, can you open your phone so I can jot down Richard's number? It'll save me bothering you for it later."

Janet punched in her passcode and handed the phone back to Sam. "Tyson's food is in the kitchen by his bowl. He shouldn't need anything else until the morning, just a treat and some water. Thank you again for caring for him, and for me, so well. You're a very special lady, DI Sam Cobbs."

Sam waved the praise away. "All part of the job. I'll be in touch soon. Take care of yourself. Does Richard have a key?"

"Yes, just close the door on your way out."

"Will do." Sam watched the paramedics wheel Janet out on the stretcher and waited for them to load her into the back of the ambulance, then she went back inside and gathered Tyson's dishes. She found his lead hanging up on the back of the door in the kitchen. The poor pup seemed bewildered. "Come on, you. Mummy will be back before you know it. Come and meet your new friend. You'll be safe with us, sweetie. Don't fret now." She attached the lead to his blue collar and tugged gently.

Tyson dug his heels in a little to begin with, but with gentle coaxing, he willingly went with Sam. She closed the front door, tested it to make sure it was secure, and then got Sonny out of the back of the car to introduce them.

They instantly became friends. Sam walked them up and down the lane for a few minutes and then secured them both with seatbelts in the back seat. She rang Des. "It's me. Sorry, I had a major incident to attend to next door. I've got an extra passenger with me so won't be able to come back to the crime scene, is that okay?"

"Fine by me. Fill me in another time, Sam. Gotta get on now."

He hung up on her.

"Ignorant git. You wait until I see him. Let's get out of here, kiddos. I might even stop off at the park, if you're lucky. Might as well, I'm wide awake anyway."

The drive back only took ten minutes. She stopped off at the park as promised and retrieved her walking jacket from the boot. The two dogs trotted along side by side, best pals already in such a short time. Sam had no intention of letting them off their leads, not at this time of morning. The park was well lit along the path but not by the bushes where she had a feeling most of their sniffing would take place. There was a lone figure off to the right. She headed towards the bridge, her usual go-to spot. The other person started walking that way, too, which kind of freaked her out, considering what time it was.

It wasn't until she got closer that she recognised who was ahead of her. *No, it can't be him. It can't be.* "Rhys, is that you?"

The man cast a glance over his shoulder to look at her. Their gazes locked for a few fraught moments, and then he took flight.

"Rhys, don't go. Come back, please, come back." Her heart broke all over again. Sonny whimpered and strained on the lead beside her at the mention of her former lover's name. "He's gone, sweetie. He doesn't want to know us, that much is evident."

Why was he here? At this ungodly hour of the morning? And why didn't he stop to speak with me? She shrugged off the incident and let the dogs sniff along the path for a few extra steps but then turned away from the bridge, not allowing herself to get any closer to a place that was so dear to her heart. Awash with feelings she had managed to push aside all week, she returned to the car and drove home.

Doreen was up and came to the door to check if everything was all right. "I was worried about you. I heard you drive off earlier and I've been watching out for you to come back."

"I had an emergency to attend to. A fire with a tragic ending, and then a witness was rushed to hospital." She opened the back door and let the dogs out. "Meet Tyson. He doesn't live up to his name. I've agreed to look after him for a few hours."

"He's so sweet. You have such a kind heart, Sam. I'll let you get the little man settled. Shout if you need me. Glad you're safe and well, that was my biggest worry."

CHAPTER 7

Sam woke up at around seven that morning. Her sleep, what little she had managed to get, had been disturbed and full of vivid dreams, some might even call them mini-nightmares, but she wasn't really one to exaggerate. Seeing Rhys at the park had unsettled her emotionally. She was surprised that she'd managed to achieve any sleep at all. That fateful night hit her from all directions. The destructive explosion had successfully wiped out not only her past but her future at the same time. Fair enough that Chris had been driven to take his own life, but why, oh why, had Rhys shown up when he had? But on the other hand, if Rhys hadn't arrived, would she have been caught in the explosion? Rhys had saved her and in doing so allowed his own dog to perish in the devastation that had followed.

That guilt of watching Rhys's car go up in smoke would haunt her day and night for the rest of her life. She and Rhys could have supported each other during their grief, but the loss had proven to be too great for Rhys. Forcing him to leave her high and dry in the end.

Still, she must move on, stop living in the past and speculating the numerous what-ifs filling her mind every time she slipped into bed at night. Rhys had made his feelings very clear indeed. She had called out, and he'd turned his back on her. Had it been a shock seeing her in their special place at that time of the morning? It was obvious he was still suffering from losing Benji. She was as well, whether he cared to believe it or not. But running away like that? Why? Did he truly hate her that much? Again, why? None of it was her fault. She hadn't asked Chris to show up that night, to beg her to take him back. It was because she had rejected him that Chris had felt the need to kill himself. Rhys was the psychiatrist after all, not her. He should have had a firmer grasp of the situation than she could ever manage to get her head around.

Sonny stretched out beside her, and then something crawled up the length of her body. She lifted her head to see Tyson sitting on her chest, his head cocked. "Hello, little guy. I bet you've woken up as confused as me, haven't you?" She stroked him, and he nuzzled into her hand.

"Come on, let's get you two in the garden before I have any accidents to clean up."

She spent the next twenty minutes seeing to Sonny's and his new companion's needs and then returned to take a shower. Glancing at the clock, she saw it was almost nine. After drying herself, she flung on a black work suit and went back downstairs to fix herself a quick breakfast, during which time she rang Richard to see how Janet was. He told her that the hospital had kept her in overnight to carry out further tests; the results of which would determine whether she came out today or not, but he was hopeful. Sam had then raised the point of possibly dropping Tyson off to him. Richard gave her his address and offered his thanks for going above and beyond and caring for Tyson in his mother's hour of need.

Sam had agreed to drop Tyson off within the hour. First, she would take them both to the park again, then she would make her way into the station, but not for too long, this was her day off after all. But with another major crime awaiting her attention, she couldn't just sit at home, contemplating the ins and outs of a second tragic investigation.

Tyson and Sonny enjoyed their stroll around the park. Sam found herself strangely drawn to the bridge, near to where she had spotted Rhys in the early hours of the morning. Disappointment slammed into her gut like a runaway articulated lorry. She went back to the car and drove little Tyson to be with his family.

Sam handed over the lead to Richard, along with a carrier bag containing his food and water bowls.

"I can't thank you enough for what you've done for our family, Inspector."

Sam's cheeks heated under his intense gaze. "Honestly, it was my pleasure. Tyson was the perfect guest in my home. I've just taken him for a walk around the park near me with my dog, Sonny, so he shouldn't need another one anytime soon."

"Again, I'm amazed and extremely grateful for the kindness you have shown him."

Sam shrugged. "The pleasure was all mine. Please, send my regards to your mother. Tell her I'll catch up with her in the near future. Also tell her to try not to worry about the other incident that happened next door."

"Mum told me about that. Horrendous. I've insisted that she should stay with us for a few days, if not more, when she comes out of hospital. That way I can keep a close eye on her and make sure Tyson gets his daily exercise to boot."

"Sounds like an excellent plan to me. Take care, Richard."

Sam jumped back in the car and nipped home to drop Sonny off at Doreen's for a couple of hours, then drove to the station. On the way, she debated whether to call her partner or not. With the station only a few minutes away, she decided to bite the bullet and rang him.

"Sam, is everything all right?"

She could hear the anxiety in his voice. "Calm down, everything is fine. Well, that's a bit of a fib. Another incident happened last night, I was called out in the early hours. I'm on my way into the station for a few hours because it's not in me to sit on my backside at home when a new case lands on my desk. I'm calling to give you the option to spend a few hours with me this morning. I quite understand if you have made other plans, don't feel obligated to give them up to be with me. I'll cope on my own, I just didn't want you pulling me over the coals about not ringing you, when you show up for work on Monday."

"Blimey, you make me out to be a right ogre."

"Damn, I didn't mean it to come across like that. Well? The choice is yours."

He paused for a moment and said, "Okay, I'll need to run it past Abigail first, she's out shopping, I'll give her a call now. There shouldn't be a problem. Shall I tell her it'll be until midday or one at the latest?"

"Yes, do that. I have no intention of staying longer than that on my day off. Thanks, Bob. I'll see you soon."

"I might stop off for a cake on the way. Are you up for it?"

"When have I ever turned down a free cake from you?"

"Yeah, I thought as much. Me and my big mouth."

Sam laughed and ended the call. She arrived at the station a few minutes later. Her first job was to pour herself a coffee, and then she scribbled down a few notes regarding what she knew about the second incident so far. Boy, a lot had happened since she'd first received the call from Des.

"Did you pour me one?" Bob shouted the second he set foot into the room.

"Jesus, you scared the shit out of me. Here I was, sitting quietly, contemplating the two cases, and you come hurtling through the door, shouting like a madman."

"Only making sure you were awake. Wouldn't want you slacking now, would I?"

Sam searched the desk beside her, found some paper, screwed it up and aimed it at him. "You cheeky shit. I'll have you know that I never got to my bed until gone two this morning, after I had walked the dogs."

He was in the process of pouring them both a coffee and paused to look at her. "Dogs? What dogs?"

She gave him the edited version of how her evening had panned out after she had knocked on Janet's door.

He deposited her coffee on the desk and sat in his normal chair. "Hell on earth. Is the woman all right?"

"An overnight stay in hospital should see her good. Tyson was a sweetheart, I couldn't leave him there all alone."

"You're far too soft where animals are concerned."

You don't know the half of it, matey. Why do you think I've been so upset lately? Losing Benji in the fire has had a huge impact on my life, as well as Rhys's.

"Are you all right? You drifted off there for a second or two."

"I'm coping better than I thought I would in the circumstances."

His brow furrowed. "Talking in riddles isn't going to help either. Let's have it, Sam, what's really going on in that head of yours?"

"Another time maybe. We've only got a few hours, I'd rather spend the time being productive."

He bit into his slice that oozed cream and jam out of the sides. "God, that's delicious."

"Manners! Don't speak with your mouth full." Sam opened the bag and nibbled on her cake. "I have to agree, it is divine. Right, let's get down to work. Although, maybe we should finish our treats first, given the subject matter we're about to discuss."

Bob rammed the last of his slice in his mouth and wiped his hands down his faded jeans. "All done."

"You might be." Sam pushed the cake aside and grabbed her pad, filled with the notes she'd jotted down. "Let's see. Des called me, woke me up, in fact, requested my attendance at a second crime scene. When I got there, the cottage was still pretty much intact apart from the lounge. That was down to Janet's quick thinking, the neighbour who was out walking Tyson, the little dog I cared for. She walked past the cottage, saw a blaze inside and rang the fire brigade straight away."

"Good for her, and then the shock took hold and she ended up in hospital. It's all right doing a good deed, but not at the cost of your own health, eh?"

"Exactly, she's such a lovely lady. I'm hopeful there will be no lasting effects, although going back home, walking past the crime scene is going to be a constant reminder for her."

Bob took a sip from his coffee. "So, was the cottage rented out?"

"I think so, yes. Back to the crime scene. Des couldn't really provide much information except that he had proof the two victims had been attacked before the fire took hold."

"Attacked or had they died?"

"Only the PMs will be able to give us that answer. He's going to be performing those today."

"What we're saying here is that another two people lost their lives in a cottage they were staying in, and then a fire was started to conceal the evidence?"

"Exactly." Sam groaned. "I knew what I was going to do first thing and I forgot."

"What's that?"

"Search the internet, see with whom the cottage was registered. I'll do it now." Sam removed her phone from her pocket and typed in *Hilltop Cottage*. "Now there's something I wasn't expecting to see, or maybe I was."

"Riddles again. Are you going to let me in on the secret, or should I go home now?"

"You can be such a miserable shit."

"I wonder why that is… oh yes, possibly because it should be my day off."

"Get over it, you were given the option to come in or stay at home, you chose the former. Can we get back to business now?"

"Go for it. Now that you've suitably chastised me. What have you found?"

"That the cottage was on the books of Valley Rentals."

"Why should that come as a surprise? The cottages are within spitting distance of each other. I don't suppose there are that many rental agencies in the area, or am I missing something?"

"Maybe you're right. Isn't there a national database for rentals? I think there are a few I can mention off the top of my head. I'm listening to my gut here, and it's telling me this has to do with the agency."

"Whoa! How can you say that, at this early stage?"

She flung her hands up in the air. "I don't know. What I'm not prepared to do is ditch the idea, only for it to come back and bite me in the arse later."

Bob sighed. "I see your point. It's not like we have anything else to go on, is it?"

"Nope, not until we have the results of both PMs back, or should I say all four of them? Des is going to be under a lot of pressure on this one."

"He's professional enough to cope with it. He'll probably have to rely heavily on his assistant to get everything tied up early. That isn't going to be a barrel of laughs for either of them."

"Not our problem. We all have our hurdles to cross. Ours is to find out why holidaymakers are being targeted in our area," Sam said.

"Good luck with that one. There could be any number of motives involved. Locals getting pissed off with the tourists coming here for a start."

"Really? Why now? The Lakes have been a popular tourist attraction for years."

"Like I said, and at the risk of repeating myself, there could be numerous motives involved. It's simple, all we have to do is try and figure it out… and quickly, before we get another call to attend a third crime scene."

"Fuck, don't say that, Bob. We have enough on our plate as it is."

"Sorry, you're not the only one who has a strange feeling settled in their gut. Where do we go from here?"

"I think we should get in the car and head over to Valley Rentals, see what they have to say about all of this."

"What? You can't go over there without an ounce of proof to bash them over the head with, not if you want to keep your job, Sam."

"I know that. Stop taking everything I say and blowing it up out of all proportion. We need to pay them a visit to get the lowdown on the victims, you wally. How else are we going to contact the next of kin?"

"*You,* there's no we in that. That's why you're the inspector, in case you've forgotten."

"Not possible, not with you bloody shoving it down my throat every couple of days. Come on, sup up."

His gaze dropped to the barely touched cream slice sitting on the paper bag. "Are you going to eat that?"

"I thought I'd leave it hanging around and play a game of football with it later if I get bored."

"Ouch! I only asked. Shit your thanks as my old gran used to say. Last time I buy you an expensive cake. A jam doughnut will do next time, *if* there is a next time."

"Grumpy git. Have it if you want it, it's too early in the day for me anyway."

He didn't need telling twice. The cake disappeared within seconds, washed down with the last of his coffee. Then he had the gall to let out a satisfied belch that ripped through the incident room.

"Christ, do you have to act like a pig twenty-four-seven?"

"Yep, it goes with the territory of trying to piss you off."

She shook her head and punched him in the arm. "You've succeeded. Get your trotters working and follow me, we'll go in my car."

He laughed and tucked his chair under the desk.

FIFTEEN MINUTES LATER, Sam parked the car outside the agency. Bob entered the reception area first with Sam close behind him. The same young receptionist was there to greet them.

Sam had to search her mind to recall her name. "Hi, is it Annie?"

"That's right. Was there something you forgot to ask when you were here last week?"

"No. Is Pat around?"

"She's in her office, making a few essential calls. She asked me not to disturb her. Can I help with anything?"

"Not really. It's important we speak with Pat right away."

Annie shrugged. "I can ask, see if she's willing to see you. Take a seat, I won't be long."

Sam and Bob paced the area for a few seconds until Sam

decided to wander around the office, viewing all the cottages the agency had on offer. She was amazed how many holiday homes there were in the area. No wonder the locals were always up in arms with the lack of properties for sale. Those that did come onto the market carried a huge price tag, compared to ten or twenty years ago. She counted her blessings for finding her new home when she had, even though it had signified the end of her marriage after a few years of renovating it. She smiled, thinking of Doreen, a neighbour too good to be true and one who she had ended up relying heavily upon since her marriage had abruptly ended.

"Pat can spare you a few minutes," Annie called out from the doorway, breaking into her reverie.

"Thanks." Bob entered the office after Sam.

Pat seemed harassed and had a desk full of paperwork in front of her.

"Hi, Pat, sorry for interrupting you like this." Sam smiled. "It's important."

"Take a seat. I'm snowed under, as you can see, but I can always make time for the police. What can I do for you today?"

"Sadly, we have news of yet another incident."

Pat frowned and sat upright. "I'm not sure I understand. Care to tell me more?"

"Last night, or should I say, in the early hours of this morning, I was asked to attend a crime scene at what we believe to be another one of your cottages."

Pat slapped a shaking hand to her cheek. "No, no, no. Not again. Please don't tell me another fire has taken place, has it?"

Sam sighed and nodded. "I'm afraid so. Hilltop Cottage."

Pat's hand slid up her face and through her greying hair, and the colour drained from her cheeks. "How… did this happen? Why? Oh my, those poor people."

"One question at a time. The how was that we believe the fire was intentionally started to cover a crime scene." Sam was fed up of holding back. The gravity of the situation was immense, and she needed to get her point across if she was to prevent any further incidents of this nature happening in the future.

"I don't understand."

"The victims were murdered at the cottage, the same as the Mansells."

"What? Why wasn't I made aware of this at the time?"

"Because we needed to get our facts right."

"Murdered. Why? Do you have the killer?"

The door opened, and in walked Annie with three mugs. "I'm sorry, I took the liberty of making you all a drink. I hope that's okay, Pat?"

"Good girl. I'm in desperate need of that."

Sam smiled at the efficient young woman. "Thanks, that's very thoughtful."

"Always a pleasure. Are you all right, Pat? You look a bit pale." Annie's gaze flicked between them, her brow furrowed with concern.

"Take a seat, Annie. Is it all right if she sits in with us? Annie is usually the face of the agency anyway, most of the time."

"I'm not averse to her being here, if you're not. Let me recap what I've told Pat."

Annie dragged a chair from the corner and sat closer to Pat than to Sam.

"I was called to attend another fire at one of your cottages last night," Sam said.

Annie gasped and placed a hand over her ruby lips. She dropped it and stared at Pat. "No way. I can't believe this."

"I know. I feel exactly the same, Annie. What are the odds of it happening twice within a week? I can assure you,

Inspector, we've never had any such tragedies to deal with before. I'm shocked and appalled to learn of this news. Shocked!"

"It is the worst news possible," Sam said. "We're going to need your help again. The next of kin have a right to know what's occurred. I'd like to get that organised with the local police ASAP, if possible. Can you give us the necessary details?"

"The Greers were such a lovely couple. Really looking forward to their time in the Lakes, spending alone time with each other. This is unthinkable. How sad they should both die in a fire. My heart goes out to their loved ones. Do you want me to find their registration details, Pat?" Annie asked, her voice barely above a whisper.

"Yes, the sooner we can give the inspector the details the sooner she can deal with the next of kin," Pat replied.

Annie left her chair and exited the room but left the door open.

"I can't believe two more people have lost their lives, how is it even possible?" Pat sighed.

"Has anyone threatened you in the past, Pat?"

"What are you saying? That you think these people have died because of me? How dare you even consider that to be the case? I'm mortified that you can come here and suggest such a thing."

Sam held her hands up in front of her. "No offence intended, I assure you. It was a simple question that any investigating officer would be at liberty to ask during such a case."

"No, I've never had a problem with anyone before," she bristled.

"What about rival agencies, are there any in the area?"

"Yes, one or two. Sometimes we help each other out at short notice with an available property for a desperate customer. I wouldn't class them as rivals, not really. There's room enough for all of us in this area, it's a thriving market." Her gaze dropped to her hand. Twiddling a pen through her fingers, she added, "Once news gets out about these two accidents, I can't help but wonder what state my business will be in this time next month."

"Hardly accidents. We've recognised them as major crimes, murder and arson. We're going to need the names and addresses of any other agencies in the area, say within a twenty-mile radius."

"I can get that sorted for you now. I'll be right back." Pat rose and left the office.

"We're getting nowhere fast here. I thought this would be easier," Bob mumbled.

"Give them time. The shock is probably taking its toll on both of them."

Bob slouched in his chair and crossed his arms. "If you say so. Something tastes and smells well off to me."

Footsteps sounded outside the office. Sam nudged Bob's leg with her own, warning him to sit up.

Annie breezed into the room and handed a sheet of paper to Sam. "The next of kin details. Can I get you another drink?"

"We're fine. Thanks for this."

"Always happy to help. Do you need anything else from me?"

"I don't think so." Sam peered over her shoulder, keeping an eye open for Pat's return. "A quick question about Pat. What's she like to work with?"

Annie frowned and scratched the side of her face. "Hit and miss, but mostly I don't have a problem with her. May I ask why?"

"I like to form a picture of those I'm dealing with. She's gone off to get the details for the other agencies in the area.

Do you have them filed away somewhere?" Now that she'd had time to think things over, Sam had trouble believing that Pat would have needed to leave her office to find the information. *Wouldn't it be available on her computer? She could have looked up the names and addresses online, couldn't she?*

Annie shook her head and pointed at the computer. "It's all in there. How strange. Let me go and find out what's going on. I'll be right back."

Sam waited until the young woman left the office and then leaned towards her partner and whispered, "Exactly what was running through my mind. Why didn't she just log in to her computer to give us the details?"

"Fishy."

"Very. I'm going to make an appearance out there, see what's going on."

"Be careful."

She jumped out of her seat and walked into the outer office where she found Annie consoling a sobbing Pat. "Is there something wrong?"

Both women stared at her but said nothing.

"I can't help if you won't tell me what's going on."

"I'm sorry. The past week has been fraught, and now, you come here and tell me that another couple of our guests have been murdered. I'm sorry but I had to come out here. I've been told by my doctor to avoid any unnecessary stress. I found sitting in the office, under interrogation, far too stressful for me to cope with."

"I was merely asking you a few questions, as is my right in the circumstances, Pat. If you'd rather take this down the station, that's fine by me."

Pat's breathing came out in short sharp breaths. In between, she muttered, "I know… I couldn't face that. Please, I'll be all right in a moment or two. I'm in shock and overwhelmed by all of this."

"I don't wish to come across as heartless, but I have a job to do. This agency is the only connection we have with the victims. We're bound to come here asking questions that you might not want to hear. You're going to have to bear with us on that one, Pat. Any information you can supply will be in both of our interests. You do want us to catch the culprit, don't you?"

Pat swiped at the tears sitting on her cheeks. "Of course I do. What sort of question is that?"

"A logical one in my opinion, considering how you're reacting."

"Well, pardon me for being overwhelmed and upset by this whole debacle, if you can call it that. Oh, I don't know... my doctor has insisted I should avoid any unnecessary stress, and here you are, heaping it on me. I don't think I can cope... not any more."

"I'm sorry you feel that way. As stated already, you're our only connection with the victims. If, however, you can't supply us with the answers to our questions, then that sort of thing throws a cloud of suspicion over your head."

"Oh no, Pat, you can't allow this to happen," Annie pleaded. "I told you, the inspector is only here asking these probing questions because it's her job. You mustn't take things so personally."

"Listen to Annie, she's talking a lot of sense. We can either work together or..." Sam agreed.

"I will. I'm sorry. I couldn't stand you thinking that I would have anything to do with these deaths. Never in a gazillion years would I ever harm someone intentionally, you have to believe me, doesn't she, Annie?"

"Yes. Pat is not capable of hurting anyone."

"Ladies, ladies, you really have got the wrong end of the stick here. I'm not accusing you of being involved in the crimes, all I'm trying to ascertain is if someone you know might be to blame, as in one of your competitors?"

"I'm glad to hear it. But I doubt if anyone we know would be as callous and heartless enough to want to kill someone, let alone four people," Annie offered.

"Do you have the information I requested?" Sam pushed, now that Pat's tears appeared to have dried up.

"I'll get it for you now." Pat set off across the office towards the filing cabinet in the corner.

"Does she always take everything to heart?" Sam whispered to Annie.

"Yes. This business means the absolute world to her. It's her baby, she has always wanted children, but the right man never came along."

"Ah, okay, now it's all making sense. What about you?"

"What about me?" Annie queried.

"Can you think of anyone who might be responsible for the murders and arson attacks?"

Annie shook her head and puffed out her rosy cheeks. "Not off the top of my head. Who knows what goes on in someone's mind? Covid has a lot to answer for in one way or another, don't you think? Are you seeing an increase in crimes of this nature since the lockdown?"

"I wouldn't necessarily say of this nature, but yes, on the whole, the crime rate in this area has increased steadily in recent years. Whether that can be directly attributed to Covid, I don't think anyone would be able to say for sure."

Pat rejoined them and held out a piece of paper. "There are two within the radius you mentioned. Lakes Cottages and Happy Holiday Rentals."

"That's great news, thanks for the information, Pat. How are you feeling now?"

"A bit better. I suppose I'm a touch overwhelmed both

personally and professionally at present, and it's beginning to have a negative effect on me."

A knowing glance shot between Annie and Sam.

"I understand," Sam said. "I was just asking Annie if she could throw any light on why someone might be targeting the agency. What about a former employee"

"And what did you say, Annie? Did anything come to mind?"

"I'm in the process of trying to think, Pat." She clicked her thumb and forefinger, startling her boss. "Sorry, I didn't mean to make you jump. What about…? No, it's too foolish to even consider."

"What is?" Sam urged.

"I'll say one name: Maisie Frank," Annie said.

Pat gasped. "Yes, oh, there's a possibility… hmm… would she? I'm not so sure now."

"Maisie Frank?" Sam asked. "Who is she? Did she work for you?"

"Oh no. She was the lady who ran Happy Holiday Rentals for several years. We used to be very good friends at one point."

"What happened to change the friendship?"

"This business grew very successful. Actually, it was around the time Annie came to work for me. She's super-efficient and really puts the customers at ease. It was her idea to make sure that she was available to welcome the guests when they arrive at a property. Of course, our rivals found out about the game-changing idea and started copying it. But no one meets and greets like Annie does. She's very attentive and sympathetic to our customers' needs, aren't you, dear?"

"I try to be. I rented a cottage down in Cornwall once and was treated like a princess. It made my holiday. When I ran the idea past Pat, she wasn't too enthusiastic until I showed her the reviews the rental agency in Cornwall received on Trip Advisor. Most of them stated that the unrivalled welcome and gift package got their holiday off to a fantastic start."

"I must admit, I've never heard of that type of service before. I can see why you do it, to help people settle into their cottages from the off."

"That's right." Annie smiled. "And our reviews have been far better since we introduced the scheme."

"They definitely have. Annie is a genius. We're all about putting the customer and their needs first."

"And what has been the reaction from your rivals?"

"They've tried to copy us but they didn't have an Annie working for them." Pat laughed. "It doesn't matter what time our guests arrive, she's always there to greet them. Supplying that personal touch to our holidays is the reason we have a ninety percent return rate."

"I see how that would make a difference to your business. On the other hand, I can also envisage it pissing off your competitors."

"Possibly. Surely that's their problem, not mine." Pat scowled.

Sam raised an eyebrow. "You're missing the point. If your competitors are pissed off enough, maybe they might stoop to drastic measures."

"Oh no, and purposefully go out and kill off our guests just to get back at us? But that's just... well, senseless. Brutally insane."

Sam ran a hand around her chin. "Worth considering. I need you ladies to think back over the last few years. Can you tell me how many times you've had negative dealings with any of your competitors?"

Pat considered the question for a few moments, but it was Annie who answered.

"There was that time when Maisie came around here shouting the odds at you, do you remember?"

"Yes. She wasn't too happy when she found out we snapped up a large family booking of twelve. Apparently, she had been in touch with the family for weeks, but in the end they decided to come with us instead. Maisie had a tendency to badger people until they paid their deposit with the company, and then she didn't want to know."

"How do you know that's the way she operates?" Sam asked, her interest mounting.

"A few of our regular customers told us that they decided to book with us because of our 'no pressure' policy. Anyway, they don't have to be concerned about that any more as Maisie no longer owns the business."

"She sold it?"

Pat nodded. "She retired back in February or March time, wasn't it, Annie?"

"Around Easter to be exact. I seem to recall she came down here for one final slanging match. She was nuts. I'm not surprised her customers felt uncomfortable dealing with her. She shouldn't have been in this business in the first place. People need to feel wanted, that they're going to be well catered for if they book a cottage for a holiday."

"Quite right. I never realised how much that was true until you started working here, Annie. I'm as guilty as Maisie in that respect. I'm glad you helped me see the error of my ways."

Annie smiled and placed an arm around Pat's shoulders and then rested her head against the older woman's. "I love working here. Making people's dreams come true when they visit the area."

Sam smiled. "I can tell how professional you both are. I'd like to have a chat with this Maisie Frank. I don't suppose you'd have an address for her, do you?"

"Sorry, we never exchanged addresses, only blows... verbal blows, I should add," Pat replied. "I would never choose to be friends with a woman like that. Maybe the woman who took over the agency can help you out."

"And it was the Happy Holiday Rentals as opposed to the other one?"

"That's right."

"You've been really helpful. Looks like my partner and I will have a full day ahead of us." Sam paused and glanced towards the office where Bob had remained and then back at Annie and Pat. "Today is supposed to be our day off, I promised him we'd only be working until lunchtime."

"Sounds to me like you're the utter professional, Inspector," Pat replied.

"I like to think so. Thanks for all the information you've given us today. We'll leave you to it now. Bob, are you ready?" she bellowed.

A dishevelled-looking Bob instantly appeared in the doorway. Sam took a punt that he had snuck in forty winks while she had been speaking with the ladies in the outer office.

"All good. Are we off now?" he asked.

Sam rolled her eyes at the two women standing in front of her and thanked them again. Outside, on the way to the car, Sam asked, "Making notes were you, with your eyes closed?"

"Umm... all right. You caught me out. I went to bed late last night, thinking I'd catch up on my rest during the day, you know, on my day off."

"I hear you. I was up until the early hours as well, chum, don't forget that nugget of information, too."

"How could I? You've told me at least half a dozen times already."

"Bollocks. You know what your problem is?"

"No, but I'm sure you're going to bend my ear and tell me."

They reached the car and slipped inside.

"You scoffed two cream cakes down that fat neck of yours."

"As if. Anyway, they were worth the risk. Where are we going? Back to the station?"

"Sorry, no chance of that happening anytime soon. We're going to show our faces at Happy Holiday Rentals."

"One of the competitors?"

"Yep. I got some valuable information out of Pat while you were in the office dozing."

"Can we move on? What about?"

"If you insist. Pat told me she fell out with the woman who previously owned the agency."

"Previously? As in she no longer runs it?"

"No flies on you, partner. She sold it around Easter."

Bob held up a hand and tipped it from side to side. "That's a long time ago. If she's to blame for the crimes, why would she do it now and not in the height of the summer?"

"Could be any number of reasons. She's been sitting at home, stewing over things that may have ticked her off in the past and decided enough was enough. Possibly leaving her retribution until the dark evenings set in. Too many risks to take in the summer months when it remains lighter longer."

"Fair enough. Can't wait to see what she has to say for herself."

"If we ever catch up with her. Pat couldn't supply an address for the woman. That's why we're heading over to the agency now."

"Makes sense to me."

CHAPTER 8

There were two people on duty at the Happy Holiday Rentals. A smartly dressed woman in her late thirties and a younger man in his mid-to-late twenties who appeared to be rough around the edges, as Sam's mum would say. The man approached them, no smile on his face.

"Can I 'elp you?"

Sam and Bob produced their IDs, and if Sam wasn't mistaken, she could have sworn that he flinched. "DI Sam Cobbs, and my partner, DS Bob Jones. Is the owner or manager around?"

"Lisa, the cops, sorry, the police are here to see you."

The woman was rifling through a cabinet and held up a finger. "Be with you in two shakes, I'm on the phone, dealing with an important enquiry."

"There's no rush," Sam assured her.

"Can I get you a drink of somethin'?" the young man asked.

"No, we're fine, thanks all the same. What's your name?"

"Why do you want to know?"

"We're making enquiries into some very serious crimes that have been committed in the area. Your name?"

He had an air of impudence about him.

He shuffled his feet and glared at her. "Tommy Philips. I ain't done anythin' wrong."

"Did I say you had?" Sam replied quickly.

Tommy moved away and sat behind the desk at the front of the office. "She'll deal with you soon. I have work to be getting on with."

"No problem."

"Jumped-up little prick," Bob muttered, loud enough for only Sam to hear.

She smiled, winked at him and busied herself searching through the rental properties on show around the perimeter of the room. "Are these all rental or are some classed as long-term lets?" Sam asked Tommy.

"Our name is Happy Holiday Rentals, what do you think?"

Bob sniggered beside her. "That told you."

"Thanks, I guess that slipped my mind when I asked the simple question. My mistake," she retaliated snarkily.

Tommy tutted and bashed his keyboard a few times.

"Right, and I'm back in the room. Hi, I'm Lisa, how can I help you nice people?"

"We're after some information."

"I'm confused. Regarding rental properties?"

"No, sorry. I should have made myself clear. We're investigating a couple of major crimes in the area. You may have seen on the local news that a cottage caught fire last weekend. Did you?"

"I did. It wasn't one of ours, thankfully. Is that why you're here? About that incident?"

"No. We're aware of who the cottage was registered with and have just come from the agency. What I would like to know is, what your relationship is like with Valley Rentals."

Puzzled, Lisa asked, "What does that have to do with the fire?"

"They think we caused it, don't ya?" Tommy shouted from behind Lisa.

She spun around and shouted at him, "Hush your mouth, Tommy Philips. Go and make yourself useful, fix us all a drink."

"I offered, they turned me down."

"Then you can make me a coffee. Go on, now."

Tommy tipped back his chair as he stood and marched out of the room.

"He appears to have anger issues," Sam stated.

"Yes, he's not the most congenial employee I've had on my books. Ignore him. I think he's had a few run-ins with the police in the past."

"Ah, that explains a lot. Before he comes back, has he ever shown any dissent or anger towards any of your customers?"

"Oh, gracious, no. I would never tolerate such behaviour. This line of questioning leads me to believe you think someone caused this fire intentionally. Is that what you're inferring?"

"Yes, we're actually investigating two similar incidents, the one from last weekend, plus there was another one that took place last night which, so far, hasn't hit the news headlines."

Lisa looked behind her and flopped into the nearby chair. "Oh heck, I had no idea. And both properties were rented out at the time?"

"That's right. Furthermore, we have evidence to believe that both couples were murdered before the fires took hold." Again, Sam was under a cloud of apprehension as to whether she should have revealed the truth about the murders or not, particularly as she hadn't informed the next of kin as yet. Not something she was looking forward to doing when they returned to the station, either. She could foresee her day getting longer and longer by the second. Still, needs must, if they were going to prevent yet another murder being committed.

"Gosh, I don't know what to say. So are you going around the other agencies in the area, warning them to make their customers aware there could be a madman on the loose?"

"Yes. Also, we're hoping to obtain further information from you about the former owner of this establishment."

Perplexed, Lisa scratched the side of her face. "May I ask why?"

"Is she still in the area?" Sam asked, ignoring Lisa's question.

"Yes, I think so. Why?"

"We have reason to believe she may be a person of interest in our enquiries."

"What? Are you telling me you think she's caused the fires?"

Sam shrugged. "When past problems arise during a conversation then certain aspects need to be investigated. We've been informed that Maisie and Pat from Valley Rentals had several run-ins a little while back."

Tommy reappeared and gave Lisa her coffee then carried on to his desk.

"This is too incredible to get my head around. I would never have thought Maisie would be capable of even considering doing such a thing. To knowingly set out to take innocent lives while their guard is down during a holiday."

"What?" Tommy shouted. "Is that why they're here?"

"You seem pretty wound up about our presence, Tommy. Can I ask why?" Sam asked.

He stayed quiet for a few seconds and then snapped back,

"Could it be because the only time we see a copper is when there's a problem?"

"Are you speaking from personal experience?" Out of her peripheral vision Sam could see Bob clenching his fists beside her. She took a step closer to her partner.

"Whatever. Filth is the filth, whether you've done anything wrong or not. You lot would rather lash out, either physically or verbally, and ask questions later, down at the nick. Never considering someone's innocence until it's too late. By that time, the damage has been done."

"That's not how it works on my watch. I'm sorry if you've had a bad experience to deal with in the past."

"Words are cheap," Tommy mumbled.

Lisa slammed a fist on her desk. "Tommy, enough of this now. These nice officers are only here trying to do their job. They've just asked a few questions so far. Why don't we cut them some slack, eh?"

Tommy shrugged and blew on his coffee before he took a sip from his mug. "Whatever."

"Do you have Maisie's address?" Sam asked Lisa.

"Of course I do. Or at least the address she used to have when she left here. I haven't got a clue if she's still there. We haven't seen nor heard from her since she sold up."

"That would be great, thanks. And since taking over, you haven't had any problems with the other agencies in the area?"

"None whatsoever. I'm not really the type to have aggro in my life. I tend to shrug it off and walk away. Life's too short to be churned up about things, isn't it?"

Sam smiled. "My sentiments exactly. Can you give us the address and we'll be on our way?"

Lisa left her seat and walked into her office. She returned carrying her mobile phone. "I'm sure I made a note of her address in my contacts. Ah yes, here we are." She offered the phone to Sam who tilted it for Bob to jot down the information in his notebook.

"Excellent. Thanks very much. And just to clarify, you've never had a problem with the other agencies since you started here?"

"Not that I can think of."

"That concludes our visit then. It was nice to meet you both."

Tommy grunted.

Sam walked past his desk and halted beside him. She waited until his gaze met hers and smiled. "For your information, not all coppers are bastards."

"Says you. That's not how I remember it."

"You're a very bitter person, Tommy. That's going to gnaw away at you over time. My advice would be for you to seek out some counselling."

His face screwed into a hateful scowl. "And you know where you can stick your frigging advice, don't ya?"

Bob took a few steps towards the vexed young man, but Sam slammed a hand into his chest.

"Leave it, Sergeant. He's not worth it."

"You need to watch your mouth and show some respect, man," Bob warned.

"Yeah, whatever." Tommy's grin was lined with sarcasm.

Sam refused to get involved further and left the office.

"Fucking toerag," Bob grumbled once he'd closed the door behind him.

"Yeah, he's been wronged in the past by the boys in blue and lashing out. We just happened to be the ones in the firing line. I don't think we should be taking it personally, Bob. Thanks for jumping to my defence back there."

"You're welcome, you know that. I believe people should speak to coppers with a civil tongue in their heads. Trouble is, the youth of today have very little respect for anyone in authority."

"A tad harsh if you ask me. You really shouldn't go around branding everyone as the same."

"If you say so. Have you finished lecturing me now? You know, what with this supposed to be my day off."

"Ooo… get you with your hand up your arse."

"Better than being anywhere near yours," he bit back and groaned instantly, regretting the words that had tumbled out. "Sorry, that was uncalled for. I take it back."

"I should think so." Sam laughed and pressed the key fob to open the door. "The address Lisa gave me is close by, although I'll have to see how close when I tap it into the satnav." She carried out the task, and the result popped up within seconds. "Five minutes away. That'll do."

"That'll give me enough time to have a snooze then."

She punched his thigh. "You dare. I need you alert for when I question Maisie."

"I'm sure you've got it covered. What are the odds she's behind the fires?"

"At this stage, I'm willing to take a gamble it's around fifty-fifty."

"I'm not so sure. That Tommy is still worth looking into, in my opinion. I'm giving it whether you want to hear it or not."

"Always willing to listen to your wise words, partner. I'm not so sure on him. If he were to blame, would he be as feisty as he was back there or would he tone it down a bit, you know, rather than draw attention to himself? I have a sneaky suspicion it would be the latter."

"But he's still worth a look at, right?"

"Absolument."

"What? First you try to bamboozle me with long words and now a foreign language. I give up."

"Didn't you learn French at school?"

"Nope… Well, that's not quite true. I attended every lesson of that class, but none of it sank in. Hated learning a foreign language, didn't see the point in it."

"One of my best friends lives in France now. She hated learning French at school, regrets not at least attempting to pick up the basics."

"How can she possibly live in another country if she doesn't speak the lingo? That's just bizarre."

"She's married to a Frenchman."

"Ah, okay, well, that's a different story. Where does she live, north or south?"

Sam started the engine and pulled away. "Somewhere in the middle, I think. In one of the wine regions. They bought a small vineyard and are making a name for themselves in the wine industry."

"Nice. Not that I drink it. It's bitter all the way for me. I might have a lager at home now and again."

"I used to enjoy a glass of wine with Rhys. He was a bit of a connoisseur." Her thoughts were filled with him talking her through the intricacies of each wine-making stage and the different grape varieties. She was still none the wiser, but her heart had leapt just listening to his knowledge over the months she'd known him.

"Are you listening to me?"

She shook her head to rid herself of the distracting images. "Of course I am. What did you say?"

"It doesn't matter. You were away with the bloody fairies, in a world of your own, as usual."

"I was *not*. That's totally unfair. I have a lot going on in my mind right now, so stop having a go at me."

"Whoa! Stop snapping my head off. I'm sorry, I forgot I need to walk around on eggshells in your presence."

Sam sighed. "No, it's me who should be apologising. There's something I haven't told you."

He sat forward and stared at her. Sam stopped at the lights.

"What's that?" he asked.

"When I agreed to look after that dog, I stopped off at the park with Sonny and Tyson. The same park where Rhys and I used to take the two dogs… and… he was there."

"Never. What happened?"

"He ran off."

"What? Without talking to you?"

"Yeah, I felt both foolish and upset that he could see me and take off like that."

"Jesus, how dare he treat you like this? If you want my opinion, you were far too good for him in the first place."

"How can you sit there and say that when you don't even know him?" she shouted defensively. The lights changed, and she drew away.

Bob huffed out a breath and folded his arms. "It was my opinion. My guess is that you only started seeing him on the rebound."

"You do spout a lot of shit."

"Do I? I don't think so."

"How could I have been on the rebound when I had fallen in love with him while I was still married to Chris?"

"What? You never told me you were having an affair. If I'd known that I wouldn't have come down so heavily on Chris."

"I wasn't, not as such. It's complicated and something I'd rather not get into just now."

"Why? You're the one who brought up the subject."

"I know, and it's my decision to end the conversation before we both fly off the handle."

"Suits me. Take a right here."

"I heard the satnav's instructions." The car fell silent. Sam sighed. "I don't want to fall out with you about this, Bob. I need space, time to sort through the gamut of emotions I'm dealing with. You know, what with organising my husband's funeral."

"Soon-to-be ex-husband's funeral, you mean."

"Don't twist my words. I'm going through a tough enough time as it is, without having to watch or correct every sentence I say to you."

Bob shrugged and failed to react verbally. That was a sign of just how pissed off he was, so Sam decided to give the subject a swerve.

THE HOUSE WAS DETACHED and very grand, tucked back at the end of a small cul-de-sac with a small woodland area at the rear, from what Sam could make out. "Looks a nice place. A quiet, respectful community."

"It's okay," Bob muttered.

"Are you going to be in a strop for the rest of the day?"

"I'm not in a strop, I never have strops."

"If you say so. Let's get this over with, go back to the station, and then you can tootle off home."

"Why? Will you be doing the same?"

"Nope, I have a lot on my plate to deal with and I can do without your miserable face hanging around."

"Charming. May I remind you that I have given up my morning off to be here with you, and this is the thanks I get."

"Stop it, Bob. I can do without the hassle. Are you coming in or would you rather stay out here and sulk?"

"The latter, but I know that's not going to happen."

Sam leaned forward and bashed her head on the steering wheel a few times. "Give me strength."

He laughed and opened the passenger door. "Are we

going to get this over with or are you going to sit here and punish yourself all day long?"

She growled and caught up with him at the wrought-iron gate of the house. "You can be so infuriating at times. How Abigail puts up with you, I'll never know."

"She loves me. Enough said."

Sam led the way up the concrete path to a solid oak door and rang the bell. She removed her ID from her jacket pocket in readiness. The door remained unanswered. There was no sign of a car outside the property either.

"We're out of luck," Bob observed.

Sam cast a glance back at the road and saw a silver Mercedes drawing up behind her rental car. "Maybe not."

A woman in her mid-sixties came tearing up the path towards them. "Who are you, and what are you doing in my front garden?"

"Are you Maisie Frank?"

"I am. And you are?"

Sam showed the woman her ID. "DI Sam Cobbs of the Cumbria Constabulary. Would it be possible to have a word with you in private?"

"Now? Couldn't you have made an appointment? Since I retired my days are pretty full. Chocka, in fact."

"It will only take a few minutes. We'd be grateful if you could see us now. It was lax of me not to call ahead and make an appointment, please accept my apologies." Sam sensed that sucking up to the woman now could likely pay dividends for them in the future.

"Very well. I won't be offering you a cuppa, though. You're lucky to catch me. I only popped back because I left my notebook at home. I was attending a WI meeting at the community hall up the road."

"We won't keep you for long, I promise."

"Come in then and make sure you wipe your feet. Better

still, take your shoes off. I've just invested in a new carpet for the hallway."

"Of course."

Maisie opened the door, slipped off her shoes and barred the hallway with her stout frame until Sam and Bob had removed their shoes. Then she allowed them to follow her into a large lounge full of what appeared to be antique furniture. Sam admired the stunning grandfather clock standing in the corner of the room.

"Like it? It was my great-grandfather's. Around three hundred years old, so I've been told."

"You need to get it valued on that show on TV," Bob said.

"Why would I want to do that, young man? I never intend to sell it and I can't see someone breaking in just to whisk it away. It weighs a ton. They were built to last in those days, not like the tat you have in the shops today. Makes me cringe to think all these antiques might be thrown in a skip one day, when I'm dead and buried. My family have already made it clear to me that they have no intention of caring for them."

"How awful," Sam said. "If ever you do want to sell it in the future, I'd be interested in buying it. It would sit proudly in my cottage."

"It'll never happen. I refuse to part with it. Right, enough small talk, I have somewhere I need to be, so I suggest you get on with why you're here."

"Would it be okay if we take a seat?" Sam pointed at the burgundy-coloured chesterfield sofa that was possibly thirty to forty years old but still in immaculate condition.

"If you wish." Maisie sat in the armchair matching the sofa opposite.

Bob withdrew his notebook, and Maisie pounced on him.

"What do you think you're doing? Don't you have to get my permission to take notes of anything I have to say?"

"Sorry. Would it be all right if I took down some notes while the boss talks to you?"

"I suppose so. You haven't told me what this is concerning."

"We're investigating a couple of major crimes that have taken place in the area in the past few weeks."

"And? What do they have to do with me?"

"If you'll allow me to finish. Both crimes have a connection with Valley Rentals. When we were there today, we asked if it was possible someone may have a vendetta against the agency... and I'm sorry to tell you that your name cropped up in the conversation."

"What in God's name are you talking about? How dare you insinuate I would do anything against the law? That Pat will get a piece of my bloody mind when you leave here. What a flaming cheek to mention my name."

Sam raised her hands to halt the woman's rant. "Please, it is just a general enquiry that we have to chase up. We wouldn't be doing the victims justice if we didn't."

Maisie threw herself back in her chair. "Ask your damn questions then, but first, don't you need to read me my rights?"

"No, we're only obliged to do that if we arrest you. Is there any reason why we should arrest you, Maisie?"

"What the hell are you asking me that for? I've done nothing wrong. I'm insulted that you've come to my door to accuse me of something."

"I'm not accusing you of anything, merely trying to sift through the facts we've been given. Is it okay if we proceed? What with you being in a hurry?"

"Get on with it then. What am I supposed to have done in that stupid woman's eyes?"

"We're investigating a couple of arson attacks." Sam didn't

get any further because Maisie bounced forward and leapt out of her chair.

She crossed the room and pointed at Sam. "No way. Don't even say what's going through your head. I would never sink so low. What is that woman thinking, throwing my name into the hat as a suspect?"

"In all fairness, I asked the question, and Pat gave me an honest answer. I have to say it was a reluctant one. Can you tell me where you were last night?"

"What? You can't be serious?" Maisie took a few steps backwards.

"I am. If you have nothing to hide then your alibi will check out, won't it?"

"What time?"

"Between the hours of say eight and twelve?"

"Goodness me. I was at the local pub having a meal with a friend from seven until nine-thirty, then I came back here."

"The name of the pub?"

"Ship Inn."

Bob noted down the information. "And when you returned, did anyone see you?"

"Anyone? What do you mean by *anyone*?"

Sam smiled. "Sorry, my mistake, did any of your neighbours see you come home at that time?"

"No, you're just going to have to take my word for it, aren't you?"

"Do you have any cameras in the house?"

Maisie retook her seat and nodded. "I have a video camera on my front doorbell."

"Can we watch the footage?"

Maisie sighed and jumped to her feet again. "It's in the kitchen, come with me. Excuse the mess, it's a tip. It was my intention to clear it up later, upon my return from the WI."

They walked along the corridor to a very dated kitchen at

the rear of the house. "Let's see if I can work this damn thing. Never had to look back on any of the footage before."

"My colleague could figure it out for you, if you allow him to take a look."

Bob stepped forward to lend a hand.

"That's what you need to do, I'm sure of it. Press that button there, and it should review the footage," Maisie said.

"That's right. I have the same one at home. They're good for dealing with unwanted visitors at the door when you're out," Bob confirmed.

"So I'm told. Shame it didn't inform me you were at the door on my way back. I wouldn't have bothered coming home and I could have avoided answering your absurd questions. All this is poppycock. I would never do anything against the law, and now you're insisting that I should prove it. Goodness me, and they wonder why the country is going to the dogs. I've never been treated this way before, ever."

"We're only doing our job, Maisie, please don't take things personally," Sam replied, throwing water over the woman's understandably sour mood.

"There. Stop it there. See, that's me inserting my key in the door at nine forty-five. Do you believe me now?"

"I do. Thank you for clarifying the situation. What about last Saturday, where were you in the evening?"

"I'll need to check my diary. I'll leave you to trawl back on the footage, it'll take a while to rewind it that far back. I won't be long." She chuntered her disappointment and walked up the corridor to fetch her diary.

"Not a happy bunny, is she?" Bob announced.

"Far from it. What's the likelihood of her being involved?"

"Hard to tell. She looked offended when you asked her for her alibi. Of course, that could all be bravado. You know what you women are like..." His head sank lower, and he fiddled with the control, anything to avoid eye contact.

Sam jabbed him in the side. "I've told you before about letting that mouth run away with you. You're doing it again."

"I'm speaking the truth, that's all. You women are experts at fluttering your eyelashes and getting your way with us men."

"What utter shit you speak with that forked frigging tongue of yours."

Maisie appeared behind them. "Here it is. Last Saturday, you said?"

"That's right."

Maisie flipped through several pages in her A6-sized notebook and then prodded the page with her finger. "Let's see. Here we are. Oh yes, it's all coming back to me now. I went over to visit my friend, Ellie, in Windermere for the evening, we took in a show."

"If you wouldn't mind giving me her number."

"I'll jot it down, although why you can't just take my word for it is beyond me. I've never had to prove myself before in my sixty-six years on this damn earth. But if it will get you off my back." She scribbled a number down and handed the torn off sheet to Sam. "Ellie's number, as requested."

"You're too kind. I'll just step outside and make the call now."

"Be my guest. The back door is open. Maybe I should keep it shut in the future. Who would have thought it, arson attacks in this area?"

Sam smiled and crossed the room. She opened the half-glazed door and closed it behind her. She strolled around the pretty courtyard garden while she rang Maisie's friend. "Hello, is that Ellie?"

"It is. Who is this?"

"My name is DI Sam Cobbs, I'm at the home of a friend of yours, Maisie Frank."

"Oh no, the police. Has something happened to her? Is

she all right? I can't come over, I have visitors this afternoon. Tell her I can visit her tomorrow."

"Please, Ellie. There's no need for that. Nothing is wrong with Maisie, so let me put your mind at ease on that front."

"Goodness, then pray tell me why you are calling me. You have fair frightened the damn life out of me."

"Sorry, please forgive me. I'm ringing to see if you can vouch for the fact that you were with Maisie last Saturday evening?"

"Yes, our local theatre was putting on a show we were both eager to see, and I arranged to get us tickets."

"In Windermere, is that correct?"

"Yes, that's right. What's this all about? Has Maisie broken the law? Is that what you think?"

"No, she hasn't. You've been most helpful. Sorry to disturb you." Sam ended the call, cutting off the woman's objections, and went back into the kitchen. "Don't bother with the footage, Sergeant. It's been verified. Thank you for speaking with us today, Maisie, we're truly sorry for the intrusion."

"Is that it? You weren't prepared to take my word for it, but you'll take the word of my friend over the phone? Un-bloody-believable! That's what it is! Grossly unfair to come here and verbally beat up a pensioner."

Rather than get into an argument with the now infuriated woman, Sam smiled and said, "Thanks again for your time. We'll let you get back to enjoying your day now."

Sam and Bob returned to the front door and put their shoes on, with Maisie still ranting in their ears. Once they left the house, the door was slammed shut behind them.

"I guess you're off her Christmas card list." Bob chuckled and led the way back to the car.

"I'd rather deal with things as they come up, it'll ensure

the investigation runs smoothly. If that pisses people off along the way, tough."

"Back to the station now, is it?"

"Yep, I have the daunting task of arranging for someone to contact the next of kin down there, now."

The doors clunked open, and they climbed into the car.

"What do you want me to do when we get back?"

"If you want to stick around, I'd like you to do the background checks on Lisa and Tommy, see what shows up, especially where Tommy is concerned."

CHAPTER 9

Sam walked out of her office and crossed the room to the drinks station. She poured them both a coffee and deposited a mug on her partner's desk.

"Thanks. How did it go?" Bob asked. He leaned back in his chair.

Sam sighed and perched on the desk behind her. "Harrowing. There's no other word for it. I've been in there the last thirty minutes making the arrangements to destroy two families' lives."

"Never an easy thing to do. How are you doing personally? All this must be having an impact on you. It suddenly dawned on me a little while back how traumatic this case must be for you to deal with, in the circumstances."

Sam took a sip of coffee and shuddered. "Don't drink it, I forgot the sugar." She returned to the drinks station with the two mugs and popped a spoonful of sugar in each, after which she rejoined her partner, handed him the mug, pulled out the chair at the next desk and flopped into it, her drink sloshing on the floor. "Damn. I can't say I haven't considered a connection. At one point, I wondered if the first crime was personal."

Bob took a sip from his mug and nodded. "Understandable. And now?"

"I think I've realised how foolish that notion was, at least I hope so. It would destroy me to think I could be to blame for four innocent people losing their lives."

"I'm glad you've managed to see sense. This has nothing to do with you, not personally."

"Thanks, partner. Enough about me, how did you get on?"

"I've picked up on something interesting with Tommy."

Sam's ears pricked up. "Go on, surprise me. What was he in prison for?"

"ABH. He was inside for two years. Here's the thing that caught my attention: I had a sudden urge to find out what type of record he had on the inside, and to my surprise, he had a penchant for setting fires in either his cell or in the recreational room."

"He did, did he? Now that's interesting. We should question him further about his antics." She watched him eye the clock on the wall. "On Monday, yes? You can get off after you've finished your drink. I'm going to hang around, work through a few things and call it a day in a couple of hours."

Bob screwed his eyes up. "You wouldn't be as daft as to go back out there and question Tommy Philips yourself now, would you?"

"You're right, I wouldn't. I said we'll do it on Monday and I meant it. No, I need to make contact with one of our colleagues down in Brighton, see if they'll do some digging for me. I also want to give Alan a call, make him aware of the second incident and ask him if he'll do some extra digging. Maybe the couples knew each other."

"It's a long shot, but worth checking, I suppose. Okay, I

won't argue with you. I think Abigail wanted to go to the DIY store this afternoon."

"Ouch, that sounds like she has a job lined up for you."

"Yeah, daft mare saw something online the other day, one of those TikTok videos about revamping the furniture in your bedroom, and had a brainwave."

"About what?" Sam had to suppress a giggle.

"We've got a range of horrible slatted wardrobes that she's always nagging me to do something about. I looked at replacing the doors with nice oak ones and changed my mind pretty damn quickly when I saw the costs involved, nearly five hundred quid a door. They can sod off. My dad came up with the idea of putting a sheet of hardboard over the top, decorating it with beading, and painting them. He even offered to lend a hand."

"Good old dad, where would we be without them, eh? By slatted, do you mean louvered?"

"That's the one, I couldn't be bothered to search for the right word."

"I gathered." She laughed. "I hope it doesn't prove to be too intimidating a task for you. I'm sure you're more than capable."

"It's not beyond my DIY skills. I've even bought an electric planer, just in case it's needed."

Sam chuckled. "Nothing like being prepared. Right, you get off when you're ready. I'll get on with making the calls in my office. I'm more comfortable doing that sort of thing in there."

"Is that your way of saying you need some space and that you're sick to death of my company?"

Sam grinned and left him to ponder whether or not his assumption was right. She closed the door and paused for a moment to take in the view. The hills had always had a calming effect over her, one that when pushed, she struggled to put into words.

Maybe when work quietens down a bit and before the weather changes for the worst, I can get some hill walking in with Sonny. Let's be honest, I can please myself what I do from now on. With no man in my life, holding me back, I can do what I want, when I want.

She pushed her melancholy thoughts away and concentrated on the business in hand. Her first call was to the station closest to where the Greers lived. It was a fair distance from Brighton itself. Inspector Mitchel Donaldson took the call.

"How can I help, Sam? It's supposed to be my day off but I got roped in to go over some old files, relating to a case we're investigating."

"Ditto. It's no fun working your weekend off. If you want to leave it until Monday, that'll be fine with me."

"Coppers don't really have a home life, do they? I should only be on this for an hour or so. I can look over what you need after that."

"Home life, what's one of them?" She laughed as a hand squeezed her heart. "That would be great. The victims' names are Shelby and Catherine Greer. They rented a cottage from Valley Rentals. Regrettably, they were murdered at the property, and the killer set fire to the cottage. We're assuming it was to cover their tracks forensically."

"Ouch! Sounds like you have a pro on your hands."

"Yep, don't think that thought hasn't crossed my mind. The problem is, this is the second incident of this nature that has occurred within the last week. The other incident took place last weekend. We've been working solidly on that one but haven't got very far at all."

"Same MO? Same company involved?"

"Yes to both. What I'm wondering is whether the couples knew each other. I did try to ask the Greers' relatives when I phoned them after they'd been informed, but they were too upset to think straight. If we can find a connection, it might put us on the right track to solving both cases. As it stands, we have very little to go on."

"I'm probably teaching you how to suck eggs here, but have you been back to the rental agency and questioned everyone there?"

"First thing I did when I came into work this morning, plus my partner and I visited a rival agency in the area to see if there was anything awry there."

"And was there?"

"Yes. But further investigation has satisfied our need to scrub round that idea. Saying that, we have a person of interest who works at the rival firm that we're going to be taking a closer look at."

"Sounds promising. What do you need from me?"

"I have another inspector working with me in the Coventry area, where the first victims lived. He's been doing some footwork for me, you know the type of thing…"

"Question friends, relatives and work colleagues, see if anything untoward has reared its ugly head in the last few months?"

"Spot on. I'm going to get in touch with Alan now. He'll probably be off duty and curse me for calling him on a Saturday, but it's a risk I'm willing to take. I'm going to dabble with the social media, see if I can find a connection between the couples there. If I come across anything, we might need to dig deeper, however, I won't be able to do it from my end."

"I'm with you. Okay, give me the names and addresses of the vics and their next of kin details, and I'll get cracking as soon as I've completed my own chores."

"Thanks so much, Mitchel."

"No problem, I'm sure you'd do the same for me if the tables were turned."

"I absolutely would." She gave him all the details he'd requested and then ended the call. After which she checked the outer office to see if Bob had left for the day. Finding the room empty, she assumed he had and resumed her seat where she booted up her computer and logged in to her Facebook account. She put the names of Shelby and Catherine Greer into the search bar at the top of the screen. Shelby had around a hundred friends. He rarely posted, a bit like her. She hated social media and struggled to keep up with what few platforms she had signed up for. Trolls were everywhere, and people were no longer allowed to voice their opinions in her view, that's why she tended to steer clear of her own Facebook page.

Feeling a little down, she moved on to Catherine Greer who appeared to be more popular than her husband. She had over fifteen hundred friends, and it looked like she kept on top of her page, posting every couple of days. Things which included funny clips and memes, but also little snippets about how married life had been treating her the past year. Sam scrolled back over the months and stopped, her heart all but in her mouth at one post in particular that pained her to read.

Shelby and I would like to announce that we're expecting our first child. We're thrilled, no, overjoyed by the news, and can't wait to welcome baby Greer to our family.

Shit, she was pregnant. Sam made a note on her pad to ensure the pathologist was told, although he was probably aware of the fact already if he'd completed the post-mortem by now.

Her stomach rolled over at the thought of that little baby never seeing the light of day. *What a heartless world we live in. So, three innocent people died in the fire, not two.*

She glanced through the friends' list but couldn't find either of the Mansells listed. Then she rang Alan Wareing to make him aware of the situation.

"Hi, Alan, sorry to intrude on a Saturday, it's Sam Cobbs up in Cumbria."

"Hey, Sam, how's it diddling up there?"

"Not too good. We've had another murder and arson attack on a cottage registered with the same agency."

"Shit! Well, that news has put a dampener on things. Two victims again. Same MO, I take it?"

"Actually, I've just surfed the internet and found out the couple were expecting their first baby, so make that three victims."

"Fuck. What the hell is going on up there?"

"I wish I knew. I'm as frustrated and cut up about this as you are. I'm stumped what to do next to be honest with you. Any suggestions gratefully received. I've just checked out the latest victims' Facebook pages and couldn't see anything out of the ordinary there."

"Hmm... you won't have access to their messages, though, will you? Might be worth a look at. Where were the latest victims from?"

"Brighton area."

"And you've got a detective helping you out down there?"

"I have. I'll ring him back, see if he can get his hands on their laptops or computers. Good thinking."

"I think too many coppers, and this isn't having a dig at you, I should correct that, *some* coppers don't tend to look further than their noses where social media is concerned. I'm guilty of learning the hard way. I missed a conversation that broke the case once, I've never made that same mistake again. Now that you've raised the point about SM, it reminded me of that one mistake. I'll do what I can at this end."

"Thanks. If we can't get access to the computers or phones, do you have any clout at Facebook?"

"Er, that would be no, I've yet to meet a copper who has. They're a closed shop for getting information."

"Think they're above the law most of the time, so I hear."

"Yep. The words blood and stone come to mind. Leave it with me, Sam. Enjoy the rest of your weekend, or try to."

Some chance of that happening. "You, too, Alan. Thanks again for going the extra mile."

"You've got this, Sam. We've got this. Hopefully we'll get the investigation wrapped up in no time."

"I wish I had your faith. Let me know if or when you find anything. Take care."

She ended the call and then promptly rang Mitchel back before he left the office. "So glad I caught you. One thing I wanted to ask… umm, request, is that you ask the next of kin for their permission to search the Greers' computers and phones. Thinking about it, their phones are likely to be with the forensics team up here and were damaged in the fire."

"Any specific reason, Sam?"

"I've had a quick flick through their social media accounts, found out something heartbreaking…"

"Oh, dare I ask what?"

"Catherine was pregnant. That makes three lives lost in the fire instead of two."

"Shit! I wasn't expecting you to say that. I'll be sure to check with the families. Is there a way around it if we can't get access to their computers?"

"I'll have to run it past Forensics, see if they can help me out. Do your best for me. Check both email accounts if you wouldn't mind, too."

"On it now. I've got your number, I'll be in touch soon."

"Appreciate it, thanks, Mitchel."

Sam ended the call and sat back to ponder the case. They had no further leads to go on, except...

SAM PULLED up outside the Happy Holiday Rentals at around four. Tommy was adjusting some of the property particulars in the window, and his face clouded over when he saw her get out of the car and approach the front door.

"You're back," he said, his tone full of irritation.

"I am. Is Lisa around?"

"In her office. I'll get her." His gaze ran the length of her body.

Sam struggled to put her finger on what was behind the look. Once he turned his back on her, she gave an involuntary shudder. He definitely had the knack of making her feel uncomfortable in his presence. Maybe that was his intention.

Should I have come alone? It's too late to start worrying about that now.

Lisa came rushing out of the office. She had a cautious smile set in place. "Hello again, Inspector. How can I help?"

"I'd like a private word with Tommy, if you don't mind, Lisa?"

"Me? What the...?" Tommy shouted behind Lisa. "Ah, I get it, you've been sticking your nose in my record down at the station, ain't ya?"

"I have to follow up on the evidence put before me, Tommy. I have a few questions to ask you."

He flung his hands up in the air and paced the floor. "I've fought hard to change my life around, and it still doesn't stop you fuckers jumping on my back every five minutes. People do change, you know?"

"I'm aware of that, and I swear, I'm not here to hound

you." Sam couldn't help feeling sorry for the young man. He had a right to feel aggrieved, to believe she was harassing him, even if that wasn't the case.

"Listen to the inspector, Tommy. It won't make a difference in my opinion, if that's what you're worried about. We have a good rapport, despite us having a few differences. Give her a chance, eh?"

The young man flung his arms up in the air again and then folded them tightly and tapped his foot.

"Why don't the pair of you go in my office? I'll take over out here for a while," Lisa suggested.

"Thanks, that would be great. Tommy?" Sam smiled at the young man.

"Whatever," he replied and turned on his heel. He stomped into the office.

"Thanks, Lisa. We shouldn't be too long. I need to follow a trail, that's all. It'll probably come to nothing, but I wouldn't be doing my job properly if I ignored the obvious."

"I understand. He's a good lad, if you'll kindly bear that in mind. He's come on leaps and bounds in the past couple of months, it would be a shame to unravel all that hard work."

"I agree." Sam walked into the office to find Tommy slumped in Lisa's chair, his face as dark as it had been when he'd first seen her draw up outside. "Thanks for agreeing to see me in private. I'll make this as painless and as quick as possible."

"Good. We shut at four-thirty, and I still have several shutdown procedures I have to carry out before I can think about going home."

"Two minutes, that's all it will take me to ask a few questions."

"You'd better get on with it then, hadn't you?"

Sam sat in the less comfortable chair opposite him. "Can we start again? I'm not really one for confrontation, Tommy."

He shifted in his chair and sat up. “I'll give you a chance if you promise to do the same.”

Sam raised a hand. “Hey, that's fine by me.”

“Right, you'd better tell me why you're here then.”

“As you know, I'm the Senior Investigating Officer on a couple of vile crimes that have taken place in the last week. I'm not going to lie, after my partner and I left here earlier, we went straight back to the station and checked out your record.”

He sat forward and opened his mouth to speak.

“If you'll let me finish… it was only because you were so off-hand with us that it sparked our interest enough to dig into your background.”

“So it's my fault, is that what you're saying?”

Sam raised an eyebrow. “My advice would be to tone your attitude down a bit. All you're doing is drawing attention to yourself, in a negative way.”

“Thanks for the words of wisdom. Just get on with it and tell me what you want.”

Sam sighed, annoyed that he wasn't prepared to listen to her advice. “Your record made fascinating reading today.”

“Did it really? You don't say. And?”

“And, it made me want to come back here and check out a few details with you.”

“I was banged up for ABH, what's there to check out? I've told you, since coming out of prison I've been a model citizen to turn things around.”

“It's not the crime you did time for that necessarily caught my attention.”

He frowned. “Am I supposed to know what you mean by that? Why do your sort always have to talk in riddles?”

“Okay, cards on the table… it's the fires you started in prison that set the red flags flying.”

His eyes widened. “What? And now because you read that

you've put two and two together and come up with five?" He jabbed at his chest with his thumb. "You think I'm the one behind the fires at the cottages, is that it?"

Sam shrugged. "You tell me. Are you?"

"No!" he shouted. "I would never do anything like that. You told us earlier that four people had died in those fires but there were signs of foul play before that. I'm not into killing people for a living. Yes, I have a record, but that was a couple of years ago, another lifetime away. Don't do this... I ain't done nothing wrong except keep my head down and get on with making a career for myself. Prison changed me for the better, eventually. I'm not denying that I made a nuisance of myself in there to begin with, but old Charlie took me to one side and had a word with me."

"Old Charlie?"

"Another prisoner who has been in and out of prison more times than he could remember. He lectured me on what I was doing wrong. Pointed out the error of my ways and how I should change them before I got a reputation inside and brought attention to myself from the hierarchy."

"The inmates running the prison from the inside?"

"That's it. You step on their toes often enough and you soon live to regret it. Charlie talked a lot of sense. I thought things over in my cell that night and decided, there and then, that I didn't want to end up like Charlie, in and out of prison for the rest of my life."

"A wise move. It looks like Lisa thinks a lot of you."

"She does. Her brother was in and out of prison, she told me it had ruined his life and separated him from his family. She was determined the same thing wouldn't happen to me and gave me extra responsibility around here. I would never jeopardise her trust in me, I promise you."

"That's good enough for me. However, just to keep my

records straight, I'm going to have to ask you where you were last Saturday and this Saturday, in the evening."

His mouth twisted from side to side. "Let me think. Last night is easy, my girlfriend Sonia stayed over at mine. Unless you want to know the ins and outs of what we got up to in the bedroom, I wouldn't push that one any further if I were you."

Sam smiled. "Okay. And last week?"

"I'm always with Sonia, she'll back me up. Wait, no, last week we were feeling a bit flush and went to see the new Bond film at the cinema."

"There, that wasn't difficult, was it?"

"I suppose. What happens now?"

"I'll have to check out your alibis with your girlfriend. Do you have her number?"

He removed his phone from his jacket pocket and, after scrolling through it, he slid it across the desk so Sam could jot down the number.

"Have you been going out with Sonia long?"

"About a year and a half. I'm considering popping the question, you know, asking her to marry me."

"How wonderful. She'll have a good man by her side if she accepts."

His cheeks coloured up, and his gaze dropped. "Thanks. I'm sorry for being so defensive. It goes with the territory sometimes."

"I completely understand. Just try your best to control your anger if a copper comes sniffing around next time, okay? Give them a chance to get to know you first before you start kicking off, swearing blind they've got it in for you. Not all of us are the same."

"I can see that. Thanks for being so understanding. Is there anything Lisa and I can be doing to keep our customers safe from this lunatic?"

"Keep a watchful eye open. If anything sparks your curiosity, in a bad way, don't hesitate to get in touch with me." Sam passed him one of her cards and stood. "Thanks for speaking with me, Tommy. I believe Lisa, she told me you're a good man."

He followed her back out into the main office. "That means a lot, thanks."

Lisa rubbed her hands together. "All done now?"

"Yes. I want to thank you both for sparing me the time. Enjoy the rest of your weekend."

Lisa showed her to the door. "I hope you find the culprit soon."

"I'm sure we will. In the meantime, please remain vigilant at all times."

Sam was relieved she had left things on a high with Tommy. That was one part of her investigation she could close the door on. After calling Sonia who corroborated both of his alibis, she made her way home. By now, the time was four forty-five. She thought about the contents of her fridge and decided to stop off at Asda on the way for a few essentials that would allow her to make an omelette. She rang Doreen before getting out of the car to see if she wanted any shopping.

"Some milk, semi-skimmed, just the two pints should do me, Sam. We'll see you soon."

Sam hung up and collected a trolley which she half-filled, despite only needing a few essentials. She ended up buying Doreen a small bunch of chrysanthemums and a box of chocolates for looking after Sonny so well.

Sadness descended on the short trip back to the house. She hadn't got used to walking into an empty home yet, and the thought of doing just that had her breaking out in a cold sweat. *Stop being so ridiculous. I have a lot to do this evening to occupy my mind, organising the final details of the funeral for one thing.* She yawned at the prospect and turned into the road that led to her property. There, standing at the window, was a watchful Doreen. She glanced over her shoulder and spoke. The next second, Sonny had his paws up on the windowsill looking out at her. He bounced on the spot, and Doreen laughed.

Sam pulled into her usual parking spot that still had a few traces of debris from the explosion dotted around here and there that she had missed on the clean-up. After unloading the car and leaving the shopping in the hallway, Sam removed the chocolates, flowers and milk and nipped next door to collect Sonny.

"What's this?" Doreen asked when Sam shoved the gifts her way.

"A little thank you for all you do for me, for us." She ruffled Sonny's soft bob of hair.

Doreen gathered Sam in her arms, forgetting that she was holding the gifts. "You know you two mean the world to me. Have you eaten today?"

"Honestly, I can't remember if I ate at lunchtime or not. It's been a pretty full-on day."

"Come in. I've made a sausage casserole. It shouldn't be long."

"I can't keep taking advantage of you like this."

"Nonsense, you're not taking advantage. Shall we eat in the lounge on our laps?"

"Sounds good to me. What can I do to help?"

"It'll take another fifteen to twenty minutes yet. Why don't you take Sonny for a walk first? The weatherman is predicting a heavy downpour this evening."

"Good idea. Come on, boy, let's find your lead. We'll be back soon."

Sam took a leisurely stroll around the block with her

faithful companion pulling her to a stop as he cocked his leg at every lamppost he came across.

Her thoughts soon drifted to Rhys and the wonderful times they had shared walking Sonny and Benji together. By the time she returned to Doreen's she was a blubbering mess.

Doreen took one look at her and hugged her. "There, there, it'll all be over soon enough, child."

"Will it? I'm not so sure."

"Come and sit down. A good comfort food dinner is just what you need to make everything right again."

With her appetite now dulled, Sam reluctantly sat in one of the cosy armchairs next to the fire. Doreen brought their dinners in a few minutes later. Sonny jumped up at Doreen, nearly knocking her off her feet.

"Sonny, get down. Don't be so rude," Sam shouted, louder than she'd intended.

"He's fine. I've saved him a little gravy, although it does have a lot of onions in it. The choice is yours whether you give it to him or not."

"I might pass this time round, Doreen. Yummy, it looks delicious."

Despite her hunger waning moments earlier, as soon as the casserole was placed on her lap, her stomach growled. Sam laughed, her mood instantly brightening. "I guess I was hungrier than I thought."

"Tuck in and enjoy."

Sam spent the next couple of hours eating and then chatting with Doreen. Eventually, she said, "Well, I'd better go. Oh heck, I left the shopping in the hallway. I'll have to go and sort that out. Good job it's not the height of summer. You stay there, and thank you once again for being so supportive, Doreen."

"Hush now. You're family to me, Sam, don't ever forget that."

"Ditto. I mean it. I'm still narked about Mum turning up, unannounced."

"She means well, love. Everyone cares about you."

"I know, but showing up out of the blue wasn't really what I needed. I'll give her a call and apologise. Another job to add to my to-do list."

"Be kind to yourself. You have a lot going on right now. Are you sure you went back to work at the right time?"

"Honest answer? No. But now I'm back, I need to do my utmost for the families involved in these hideous crimes."

"I have faith in all you do, Sam. You're one of the most determined and courageous women I know."

Sam leaned over and pecked Doreen on the cheek. "Thank you. I'd better go while my head is still able to fit through the door. Thanks for a lovely meal. I'll repay the favour soon, I promise."

"Bah, you don't have to do that. You have enough on your plate, excuse the pun, as it is right now."

Sam left the house with Sonny off-lead beside her. She spent the next fifteen minutes putting the shopping away, then took the plunge and sat down with her funeral file to go through the final plans. She must have drifted off to sleep because Sonny barked and woke her a little while later.

She let him out into the garden; he must have heard a cat or something. He tore down the length of the lawn to the fence at the bottom, his nose to the ground, sniffing at the base.

"Come on, do what you need to do, boy, and come in." The garden was lit by the security light, and she peered at the sky. Even though it was dark, she could see the outline of several heavy clouds gathering overhead. Then a few drops of rain splattered her nose.

Sonny continued to sniff around the shrubs for a few more minutes even after Sam had retreated to her kitchen. Eventually, Sonny's inquisitiveness to know where she was got the better of him, and he came to find her. Sam secured the house and retired to bed, exhausted by the day's exploits.

CHAPTER 10

Monday morning was spent updating the team and going through the numerous emails and letters that had dropped on her desk over the weekend.

"So you went back to the agency to speak with Tommy?" Bob queried.

"Yes, that's right. I rang his girlfriend, and she backed up his alibis. After which, I no longer wish to declare an interest in him as a suspect."

"What? He set his cell on fire in prison, numerous times. He's got history," Bob bit back.

"He explained the situation to me. I checked his record over a second time and found that all the fires took place at the beginning of his term in prison, not at the end. He told me he met a fellow prisoner on the inside who pointed out the error of his ways. He also told me he's fought hard to turn his life around, and I have to say, I believe him."

"So why did he make a show of himself? Rant when he realised who we were and the enquiries we were making?"

"Because he doesn't trust the police. Most ex-cons have the same problem, it's not uncommon for them to have trust issues. He's dealing with them. During the time I spent with him he mellowed, calmed down considerably, enough to ensure I changed my mind about him."

"Bugger, I hope you're right and he doesn't have another victim in his sights, plus, you still shouldn't have gone there alone," Bob huffed, crossing his arms.

"Your reluctance to believe in him and to question my years of experience solving cases is duly noted, partner."

"Good. I'll take pleasure in pointing the finger and telling you 'I told you so' at the end of this investigation."

Sam turned her back and murmured, "I'm sure you will." She picked up the marker pen and brought the board up to date, something she had forgotten to do on Saturday before she had left for the evening.

"Do you think the couples knew each other, boss?" Claire asked.

"I've got both the detectives I'm working with, in the Midlands and down south, searching the victims' emails and social media. I carried out a rough check on Saturday but couldn't find anything to link the couples."

"Might be something in their emails or Messenger," Claire suggested.

"Spot on, that's the assumption I came to as well. I was going to do it myself this morning, but as you're quick off the mark, I think I'll hand the task over to you, Claire."

"What do you need me to do?"

"Contact Forensics, see if they discovered the victims' phones at either of the scenes and whether we're able to gain access to any of their emails or Messenger chats. I know some of my friends refuse to have Messenger on their phones after they were hacked, not worth the risk, they said. I wish I could delete it at times."

"Me, too," Claire agreed. "Same goes for all social media, it's more trouble than it's worth."

"You won't get an argument from me on that front, either," Bob called across the room.

Sam winked at Claire, wet her finger and struck the air. "Well then, that's got to be a first, Bob Jones, actually agreeing with me about something, and in public, too. You all heard it. Maybe I should get a plaque made to stick up on the wall to act as a constant reminder."

"Ha-bloody-ha, I see you're back on form."

Sam faced Bob and smiled. "I've never been off form where ribbing you is concerned."

Claire laughed and picked up the phone. "I'll get on to Forensics now."

Sam nodded. "Does anyone else have anything to add? Any avenues that you believe we should be investigating?"

A lot of blank faces stared back at her.

"Okay, let's keep digging, something has to come our way soon."

SAM'S WISH came true that afternoon when she received a call from Alan in Coventry. "Sam, it's Alan. As requested, I went back to the family, and Tara's sister got me in to see her Facebook messages. Apparently, they both knew each other's password for the site."

"That's great news. Dare I ask what you found?"

"Interesting messages from an Annette Mitton. I'm presuming, by the gist of the messages, that she works at the rental agency."

Sam's brow furrowed. "There's an Annie there. She might go by Annie rather than use her full name. Any chance you can print off the messages and send them through to me?"

"Already sent. Want to check your emails?"

Sam tapped the spacebar on her computer to wake up her screen. She opened the email Alan had sent a few minutes earlier and scan-read the messages. "Hmm… attention-grabbing insight. She came across as a very efficient young woman when we paid the agency a visit. Pat informed us that Annie came up with the idea of meeting and greeting people at the cottages, you know, adding a personal touch that other agencies in the area failed to deliver."

"That explains her being so friendly in the messages then. She also states that she couldn't wait to meet them in person. I did wonder what that was all about. I've booked a couple of cottages in Devon before and never had any personal contact with the booking agents, just corresponded via emails. Can I draw your attention to the messages near the end?"

"I'm scrolling through, give me a sec. Ah, here we are. What am I searching for in particular?"

"Annie lays her heart on her sleeve. Says she lost her husband a few months ago. Tara shows her sympathy. She was a nurse and advised her to get some counselling to heal the wounds."

"Very interesting indeed. They do seem to get on well together. I wonder how her husband died. Something we can look into at our end, hallelujah!"

"You took the words out of my mouth, it's about time you lot up there earned your money."

"Cheeky sod. Okay, thanks for sending this through, Alan. I'll let you know later how we get on."

"Always a pleasure. I hope it comes to something."

"So do I. Speak soon." Sam ended the call and immediately rang Mitchel in Brighton. She made him aware of what Alan had uncovered and asked how he had got on with gaining access to the Greers' computers.

"I'm almost there. Shelby Greer's father was nipping over to the house for me to see what they'd left behind. I'm waiting to hear back from him."

"It's the messages we need to concentrate on." Sam logged

in to her Facebook account and searched for Annette Mitton. The name popped up straight away. There was no profile picture, but judging by the personal information, she could see it was the same person who had sent the messages to Tara. Her Facebook page was full of quotes about love and missing someone who had departed. There were a few holiday snaps, and Sam zeroed in on those and quickly identified the woman she knew as Annie.

"That's the best I can give you for now, Sam. I'll get back to you as soon as I've gained access to the house and the computer, if there's one available."

"Thanks, Mitchel, I'll be in touch soon. TTFN." She hung up and bellowed for Bob to join her.

He came flying through the door. "What's wrong?"

"I need you to take a look at this woman." She beckoned him, and he shot around the desk and peered over her shoulder.

"Bloody hell. Is that Annie from the agency?"

"It is. Alan forwarded me a printout of these messages that Annie and Tara sent back and forth to each other before the couple arrived at the cottage. Read them, tell me what you think." She gave up her chair for him to sit and read them properly. "I'll be right back." She nipped out of the office and marched over to Suzanna's desk. "Can you do me a favour and try to find out how Annette Mitton's husband died? I don't have a clue what his name was, sorry, I should have checked on her friends list on Facebook."

"No problem, boss. I can do that now."

"Thanks. Let me know the second you find anything."

Claire ended the call she was making and waved to get Sam's attention. "How did you get on?" Sam was eager to hear.

"Forensics weren't very helpful. Yes, they have several items waiting to be analysed. Two phones and a laptop from the Mansells' cottage, and similarly, two phones at the cottage rented out by the Greers."

"What's the hold up? Don't tell me, it's the fact they were damaged in the fires."

"Exactly that. They're doing their best to salvage the SIM cards, but it might take a while for them to overcome the complications."

"No worries. I think we've located the information we need anyway. Shh… that remains in this department."

Claire tapped the side of her nose. "I'll pull an imaginary zipper over my mouth if the guy from the lab calls back."

Sam laughed. "I must get back to it, see what Bob is up to in my office. I never like to leave him alone for more than a few seconds. The temptation to put a toad in my desk while I'm otherwise engaged might enter his mind. Ugh… what am I saying? That image will sit with me for the rest of the day now."

Claire grinned and got back to work.

Sam returned to see what Suzanna had accomplished in her absence. "Do you have anything for me?"

"I found a Dave Mitton on her friends list. He wasn't listed as in a relationship with her, though, so it could be her brother-in-law, perhaps?"

"Possibly. Can you do a deeper search? Has he posted recently, if not, then can you see if we've got him listed as deceased?"

"I'll check now, boss." Sam patted her colleague on the shoulder and returned to her office to find Bob shaking his head and still scrolling through the information on the screen.

"It makes interesting reading, doesn't it?"

"And some. The two-faced bitch. She looked us right in the eye and didn't even flinch. She must have frigging ice running through her veins."

"You're probably right. Hard to believe. She came across as compassionate and totally trustworthy. Still, we mustn't jump to conclusions just yet."

"Conclusions? Are you kidding me? I think any idiot can see she's as guilty as sin."

"But without evidence, how are we going to prove it?"

"Pass. I'm thinking how we can overcome this. We've still got a few things to check out regarding her background and how her husband died. I'd rather have that information to hand before we attempt to pull her in for questioning."

"Ah, gotcha. Jesus, why? How could she be guilty of such heinous crimes? My internal criminal antenna must be on the blink. I didn't suspect her of any wrongdoing at all. Maybe I should have when she screwed up the amount of sugar she put in my coffee."

"Numpty. I wouldn't complain about that, instead, I'd be rejoicing in the fact that she hadn't laced it with poison."

He scrubbed at his mouth. "Fuck! Seriously, I'm never going to accept another coffee while we're out again. It's just like you should never complain about your meal and eat a replacement a restaurant supplies. I read an article once about several dishes this Indian takeaway had delivered."

Sam heaved. "Oh God, I don't want to hear what the results were."

"You do. Sperm, urine, both human and canine, spittle, bogies. You name it, everything was in there."

Bile rose in her throat and lodged there. "Oh shit! I said I didn't want to know. I'm never going to want another takeaway for the rest of my life."

Bob pulled a face and stroked the front of his neck. "Yeah, maybe I should have sat on that information. Not my wisest move today."

"Not by a long shot, I'd say."

Their conversation ended, and a knock sounded on the door.

"Come in," Sam called out.

Suzanna poked her head into the room. "The husband died in August. It was a hit-and-run."

"Shit! Anyone arrested for it?"

"Yes. A young man in his mid-twenties. He was on holiday in the area and got frustrated sitting in a traffic queue. Dave Mitton was in a coma for a few days before the hospital turned his life support off and let him slip away."

"How sad. Still, if we're on the right track with Annie, that's no excuse to bump off the victims. Thanks, Suzanna."

"No problem, boss." Suzanna left the room.

"Why do you think she started killing people off then?" Bob asked.

"Who knows what goes on in people's minds when they've suffered such a traumatic loss?"

"A loss turns them into a killing machine, is that what you're saying?"

"No, you said that. I was simply saying that traumatic circumstances can impact a person's life in ways we're uncertain of."

"Maybe you should run the scenario past Rhys to give us a clearer idea of what we're up against here."

"Or maybe we could give one of the other dozen or so psychiatrists in the area a shout, you know, to save me having to deal with any more unwanted heartache."

Bob had the decency to cringe. "Sorry, I didn't think."

"Patently obvious, partner."

"So, where do we go from here?"

The phone rang, and Sam rushed to answer it. "DI Sam Cobbs. How may I help?"

"Sam, it's Mitchel. I've got the information you were after."

"Mitchel, that's brilliant. What did you find out?"

"At the house, Shelby's father managed to locate Catherine's laptop. I've rushed it to the lab here, asked them to do the necessary to get into the computer. I just wanted to keep you informed and to raise your spirits. They sounded like they were floundering when we spoke earlier."

"I must admit, they were. Get back to me as soon as you hear anything."

"You've got my word."

Sam punched the air. "Another nail in her coffin, maybe. Mitchel has got his hands on Catherine's laptop and sent it off to their lab. We have to await the results on that. As for what we do next, I say we put a surveillance team on Annie for now. We need to monitor her every move."

"All right if I point something obvious out?"

"Go on."

Bob ran a hand over his chin and round the back of his neck. "I'm wondering if she's likely to do anything unfavourable during the early part of the week."

Sam nodded. "Because the other crimes have both happened at the weekend? Yep, you're right. What about midweek stays, does the agency do any of those as well?"

Bob shrugged. "I should imagine so at this time of year. Less likely in the summer, I'd say."

"I agree. Let's get the surveillance organised, we'll do it in shifts. You make the arrangements, fill the rest of the team in, and I'll do some research on the agency, see if they do midweek bookings on their website. I might even give Pat a ring to find out if they have any clients arriving this week."

"Good idea. I wouldn't make it too obvious, though, if I were you."

Sam gave him one of her looks, and he backed out of the room wearing an extra-large toothy grin. She retook her seat and brought up the number of Valley Rentals and dialled it.

Annie answered the phone. Sam requested she be put through to Pat.

"Just a moment. I believe she's on the phone to a client. Ah, yes, she's free now. I'll put you through." The doorbell chimed in the background. "I'll have to go, there's a customer just come in."

"Thanks, Annie. I'll stay on the line."

"Hello, this is Pat, who am I speaking to?"

"Hi, Pat. It's DI Sam Cobbs. I think Annie had to run off to deal with a customer, I thought I heard the bell ring."

"Ah yes, she's always dropping me in it. I've warned her about pulling that stunt before. I prefer to monitor my calls properly, it's far more professional."

"I quite understand."

"Anyway, enough about what goes on around here. How can I help, Inspector?"

"I was wondering if you ever rent out your cottages midweek."

"Of course we do. Not so much in the summer, most of the property owners won't allow us to do anything less than a week because of the extra cleaning costs involved."

"I get it. Do you have any cottages booked out from Wednesday this week?"

"Yes, I believe we do. Let me check the system for you. I take it there's no news about finding the killer yet?"

"Not so far. We're going down the preventive measure route now."

"Sounds ominous. Is that why you want to know who is about to arrive in the area?"

"Yes. Any luck?"

"My, you'll need to be more patient than that, Inspector, I'm getting on, and computers, no, make that technology in general, can test me to my limits at the best of times."

"Sorry. I'm eager to get on."

"I'm sure. Ah, let me see. Yes, we have a cottage rented out from Tuesday this week until Friday."

"Would it be possible for you to trust me with the address?"

"Of course. It's Hazeldene Cottage in Seaton."

"And is Annie due to welcome the guests to the cottage?"

"Oh yes. She's arranged to meet them there at six in the evening. She won't be in danger, will she?"

"Highly unlikely. It's probably me being overcautious. The other crimes have taken place at the weekend. But I'd rather be prepared than have another couple of victims lying in the mortuary. Can you give me the names of the people who have rented the cottage?"

"Yes, it's Rosie and Jess. Ah, they're bringing a little dog with them as well."

"Thanks for the information. I'd keep this conversation between you and me, I wouldn't want Annie getting anxious and unable to perform her duties properly."

"Ah yes, that's a good shout. I won't say a word."

"One more thing before I crack on. Do you ever do rentals on a Monday?"

"Ah, rarely. We haven't had one of those in years as far as I can remember."

"Wonderful. Okay, I'll be in touch soon if anything else comes to mind."

"Good luck, Inspector Cobbs."

Sam ended the call and shuddered, icy fingers tickling her spine at the thought of another dog dying in a blaze. She couldn't allow that to happen. It was enough having one dog's early demise on her conscience, without adding to her misery. Not that a dog's life mattered more than a human's. She shook the thought out of her mind and returned to the incident room.

"Listen up, guys. We're going to need to sort out the

surveillance ASAP. I've just called the owner of the agency. She told me that there are clients due at a cottage in Seaton tomorrow evening at six p.m."

"I take it Annie is going to be there, acting as the ever-wonderful greeter," Bob said.

"She is. I checked with Pat and then told her to keep the conversation between us for fear of Annie being worried."

"What's the plan then?" Bob asked.

"I want the surveillance team to sit outside the agency and follow Annie home this evening. Any volunteers?"

Liam and Oliver glanced at each other and nodded.

"Liam and I will do it, boss."

"Thanks, that's great. Let's see if she makes any movements tonight or if she remains at home the night before, planning her attack. Stick with her until the bedroom light goes out. Ring me at home the second that happens."

"Will do," Oliver said.

"Bob, bring up the map of Seaton, let's see if we can locate Hazeldene Cottage."

Her partner switched on the large-screen TV and then brought up Seaton on the map and transferred it to the TV.

Sam got closer. "Magnify it a touch and scan the area." She took another step closer but retreated again, her eyes hurting under the glare from the screen. "There it is. Okay, it's down a country lane, like the other properties. I have a good feeling about this, or should that be a bad feeling?"

"Either way, your suspicious mind is on full alert. Looks a possible target to me."

"Okay, Liam and Oliver, why don't you head over there now? Stop off somewhere to grab a decent lunch. I'll get some money out of petty cash for you."

"Thanks, boss. We'll take your car in that case, Liam, I only had mine valeted last week."

"Get you," Liam tutted. "Sarah will go apeshit having a takeaway smell lingering in the fabric."

"Stop it, the pair of you! I meant for you to stop off at a pub or café and get a proper meal down your necks. Why is a takeaway always at the top of blokes' agendas whenever food is mentioned? Anyway, Bob can share a gross snippet of information about an Indian restaurant that will turn your stomach and put you off eating out for life."

Oliver held up his hand when Bob opened his mouth to speak. "Don't bother, Sergeant."

Sam jogged into the office to collect thirty quid from the petty cash tin and handed it to Liam. "If it's any more than that, let me know tomorrow. I'll be awaiting your call later. Actually, give me a ring when you arrive at her home. I shouldn't have to tell you to be discreet, should I?"

Both men nodded and got to their feet. They walked out of the incident room, discussing the best places in town to grab a bite to eat.

JUST AFTER FIVE-THIRTY THAT EVENING, Liam made contact.

Sam answered her mobile. "Where are you?"

"She's on the move. We've got three cars between us and are tailing her now."

"Good. Let me know when you arrive. Did you sort out some grub?"

"Yeah, we stopped off at a local pub and grabbed a burger and chips each. Can highly recommend it, boss."

She smiled. "Thanks for the tip, maybe Bob and I will try it out in the near future. Take care, don't let your guard down. She's cannier than she looks, that one."

"Don't worry about us, boss. Speak later."

Sam ended the call and tipped her head back to stare at the ceiling which was in need of a fresh coat of paint to cover the nicotine stains left by the previous inspector's incessant smoking habit. She wrinkled her nose, neither liking the smell of cigarettes nor the thought of wasting money on something that went up in smoke.

Bob poked his head around the door. "Ah, caught you napping."

She glared at him. "Hardly. What can I do for you?"

"I was wondering if we can send the team home now. There's nothing else we can do at this end, is there?"

"Yes, let's call it a day. I could do with an early one myself. I've still got the final touches to add to the funeral notes."

Bob groaned. "You're a saint dealing with that when you were on the verge of getting shot of him… I mean going through a divorce."

Grinning, she said, "A clear conscience is what I'm striving for at the end of all this. I'll still be on duty, kind of, monitoring Liam and Oliver's evening."

"I know. You never stop. Want me to hang around, or can I shoot off?"

"No, I'm fine. I'll be right behind you."

"Hope you don't get too stressed tonight."

"I won't. Goodnight, partner. Have a good one."

"I doubt it. Another trip to the DIY store is on the cards later."

"Ouch, sounds expensive."

"I hope not. Payday ain't until next week."

"You'll get it sorted with Abigail, I'm sure."

"See you tomorrow."

Sam drove home and picked up an excited Sonny from Doreen. She took him to the park, saddened that there weren't alternative options for them to go on at this time of the year. It was different in the summer, there were lots of public footpaths they could take through the fields. In October, those much-loved routes were usually under six inches or more of mud. There was no way she could risk taking Sonny across the fields in the pitch-black, unaware of what they were both treading in.

Her heart rate escalated the closer she got to her special bridge, but it sank again when she found the park empty. Her thoughts soon turned to Rhys, wondering how he was coping, being alone.

Is he working extra hours? Is he taking more time off to be at home, dwelling over things? Should I call him to check if everything is all right? No, I can't, not after last time. It's obvious he wants nothing more to do with me.

"Come on, boy, let's go home. I still have work to do." Her legs felt like they were weighted down with lead. She took longer than normal to get back to the house. After giving herself a good talking-to, she let herself in and quickly knocked up an omelette for her dinner. While it was cooking, she prepared Sonny's evening meal which he scoffed down as if he hadn't been fed in days.

Dinner made, she washed it down with a glass of white wine from the open bottle she had in the fridge and flicked through her funeral file while she ate. Of course, as the emotions rose inside, she regretted not leaving it until later. She ended up pushing her half-finished omelette away. She completed making a list of what was left to do for the arrangements, cleared up the kitchen then retired to the lounge to see what was on the TV. Other than the dire, depressing soaps that everyone in the UK seemed to enjoy watching, she found a documentary on life in the Lake District and was glued to it in no time at all. At around nine-thirty, Liam called.

"How's it going?"

"She's retired to her bedroom and switched off the light, boss."

"Anything else happened throughout the evening? Or did she remain in the house?"

"She stayed inside."

"Okay, leave it another ten minutes, in case she has a change of heart, and then go home. Thanks, guys. I'll see you in the morning."

She jabbed the End Call button just as the programme finished. "Oh well, that about sums my life up right now." She decided to get an early night herself.

Sonny ventured out into the garden to do his business. Sam filled the kettle and prepared her breakfast items on a tray for the morning. Anything to save time, she was determined to get into work swiftly and crack on with another day.

Despite her best efforts, Sam suffered yet another restless night. Eventually, she jumped in the shower at six and then gave Sonny a cuddle until just gone seven. She would have loved to have begun her working day early, but there was no way she could impose on Doreen at this hour of the morning. She checked if her neighbour had opened her living room curtains at seven-thirty—she had. Sam's pulse raced at the prospect of getting on the road earlier than normal, and after bolting down a bowl of cereal and a mug of coffee, she gathered Sonny's dinner and treats together and headed next door.

Doreen opened the front door in her dressing gown. "Want to start early today, Sam?"

"Morning, Doreen, would you mind? Today's the day we're hoping to trap the killer."

"Oh my, how exciting for you all. But dangerous, too, I should imagine."

"Yes, lots of planning to do in the meantime."

"You get off then, and Sonny will be all right with me. I'll be sitting there all day with my fingers crossed for you all."

"We're going to need all the luck we can muster. Thanks again, Doreen. See you later, Sonny."

"If you have to work longer, I don't want you to stress about putting me out. Sonny can stay with me for as long as you need. I've got his ball out back, I'll play fetch with him. I doubt if he'll miss his walk."

"You're wonderful. I can't thank..."

Doreen raised her hand. "Don't say it. Just go to work, and please, come back safely."

"I will." Sam waved and slipped into her car. The traffic was relatively free-flowing at this hour of the morning. "Good, no snarl-ups to dampen my mood before the day gets underway."

She was the first to arrive, but then both Liam and Oliver joined her fifteen minutes before their shift was supposed to begin. "You guys are amazing. I'll make it up to you, I promise. I have a feeling it might be a late one tonight. You might want to prewarn your other halves during the day."

"They'll be fine. It's not like it's a regular occurrence, boss," Liam replied.

THE DAY DRAGGED by for Sam. She was anxious to get the investigation wrapped up, but without catching Annie in the act, they had very little they could fling at her. A few messages and emails in which she'd opened up to her victims wouldn't really cut it in a court of law, Sam realised that. Which was why they all needed to pull together this evening and catch Annie doing the deed, if, and it was a massive *if*, she chose to strike again this evening.

During the morning, Sam sent Liam and Oliver to stake out the agency. The new arrivals were due at the cottage at six, therefore, she and Bob had driven out to the cottage at around lunchtime to survey the area. They identified several possible spots where the team would be able to hide, ready to strike later. The one piece of key knowledge they were lacking in respect to the first two incidents was *when* Annie had struck. Was it when she had welcomed the couples? Or had she returned to the cottages later in the evening? They were aware that neither couple had retired for the evening because all four of them were found downstairs, in the living room of each property, and from what Sam could tell, were all fully or partially clothed, by that, I mean, they weren't wearing their nightwear.

Sam brought the rest of the team together at just before five. "We all know what is expected of us this evening, don't we? We're going to head out that way soon, get into position and wait for the heads-up from Liam and Oliver as to when Annie is on her way to the cottage. Then we need to sit and wait."

"That's the part I'm having trouble getting my head around. What if she attacks the couple as soon as they arrive?"

"We'll be prepared for that."

"Will we? Maybe we should have rigged up a camera in the property to have given us a clearer idea of what was unfolding."

Sam kicked herself. Her partner had come up with a good idea, albeit at the eleventh hour when it was far too late to put into action. "And you couldn't have suggested that earlier?"

"Sorry. Maybe I should have."

Sam rolled her eyes. "I'm going to be keeping a close eye on the cottage. By that I mean, as soon as the couple and Annie enter the house, I'll make my move into the front garden and observe the proceedings from there."

"That's risky, boss," Alex stated.

She threw her arms up in the air. "It's the best I can come up with at short notice. Bob had an excellent idea but voiced it too late in the day for us to do anything about it. It is what it is, guys. We're not amateurs, we need to remember that fact. If we can pull this one off without anyone getting hurt then that'll be a job well done. Let's get this show on the road."

Two cars left the station, Sam and Bob up front and Alex and Suzanna in the following car. Claire had agreed to remain at the station and monitor the operation from there. The night was drawing in, the sunset peeked over the brim of the hills in the distance.

"That's a blessing, at least it will be dark when we all arrive at the cottage."

"Let's hope she doesn't spot the cars in the opposite field," Bob said.

"It was kind of the farmer to allow us to use it. Lucky he was around when we were out there earlier."

"Yeah, he appeared friendly enough. Most of them can be grouchy buggers, especially during the summer season."

"I'm not surprised. I bet they get sick to death of people trampling over their land and leaving gates open in the summer months, putting their livestock at risk."

"Most holidaymakers leave their brains at home... fact," Bob muttered.

"Maybe that's the reason the victims got caught out and why Annie seized the opportunity to kill them."

"Possibly. I hope it's not a late one tonight."

Sam bit down the urge to snap at him. "Why?"

"There's a good film on the box I want to see later."

Sam groaned. "Ever heard of recording it or even finding it on catch-up?"

"Too much hassle."

"If you can't be arsed then that's your lookout, buddy."

"Thanks for the sympathy, much appreciated." He sank lower in his seat and closed his eyes.

Sam had the pleasure of thumping him in the leg when they arrived at the cottage ten minutes later. Bob woke with a start and sat upright, his hands clenched into fists in front of him.

"All right, calm down, macho man. We're here. We need to get into position. Liam called, they've followed Annie back to her house."

"What time is it?" Bob rubbed his eyes to view the clock on the dash.

"Five forty-five. The couple are due at six. I reckon Annie might show up around five fifty-five, so the quicker we're in position the better. I'll have a word with Alex and Suzanna. You stay here, let me know when Liam gets in touch."

Sam left the car and gave instructions for her colleagues to put their car in the field opposite. She also pointed out a couple of suitable hedgerows to hide behind, both within striking distance of the cottage. She returned to the car to find Bob in a frenzy. "What the hell is wrong with you?"

"You got out, and a wasp flew in."

"Jesus, man, get a grip. Open the bloody door, it will soon find its way out. In case you have forgotten, the car is stationary. Any news from Liam?" Her phone rang. "Ignore that. Liam, what news do you have?"

"We've just pulled away from her house. We believe we're heading your way, boss."

"Good. We're all here, ready and waiting. Hold back, it's a narrow track. If she sees you turn in behind her she's going to become suspicious. Better still, stay on the main road. I've got a sneaky suspicion she lets the couples settle in and then comes back later to do the deed."

"Oh great," Bob complained next to her.

She ignored him and grinned.

"Will do, boss," Liam said. "We'll keep in touch."

Sam started the engine and drove through the gate into the field opposite, and the four of them got into position.

NOT LONG AFTER, a black BMW arrived. Sam watched the female couple get out of the car and stretch the knots out of their backs after their long drive. The blonde woman let a Scottie dog out to have a pee up the wall. It wasn't long before another car could be heard coming up the narrow lane. Sam peered around the bush in the front garden and saw Annie getting out of the car. All smiles, she approached the couple. She showed them into the house, switched on all the lights and conducted the tour which ended up in the lounge.

Sam's heart pounded harder. *Is she about to make her move?*

Instead of attacking the two women, Annie left the cottage, still sporting her wide smile, and jumped back into her car. Sam waited until the two guests left the lounge and Annie had driven off before she made her move. The rest of the team joined her in the field where they'd parked their cars.

"That went well, not," Bob whined.

"It's as I suspected. I'll contact Liam, let him know she's on her way back and tell him to tail her. I still believe all is not lost and she's going to return later."

"Is that you relying on your crystal ball again?" her partner quipped.

"We'll have to sit tight until Liam contacts us."

The four of them chatted. The two men had them in stitches at times, regaling them with amusing accounts of the investigations they had worked on over the years. In particular, Alex, with his dry sense of humour, had Sam bursting for the loo.

"Stop it," she said, "you're going to make me piss myself."

Two hours later, when Sam had just about given up hope of anything happening, Liam rang.

"She's left the house, boss, and get this, she's dressed all in black."

"Okay, that sounds ominous. Do as before, stay on the main road, it's not far. Can you and Oliver join us on foot once she's on the track and take up your positions around the house?"

"Will do. See you soon."

She ended the call and then hopped out of the car, the others right behind her. They made their way towards the cottage and hid in their respective hiding places. Sam discreetly hid behind the large bush in the front garden where she had an excellent view of what might take place in the lounge. The two ladies were sitting on the sofa, stroking their dog. To the left of her, headlights lit up the lane but switched off around twenty feet from the house. Sam hunkered down low, behind the bush.

A black figure rushed past her and around the back of the house. Sam hoped the others were paying attention. Liam and Oliver whizzed past her. She let out a relieved sigh to see them both safe.

The dog barked inside. Sam peered through the window and saw the masked figure in the doorway. That was enough for her. She gave the instructions for those closest to the back door to make their move.

Annie shouted at the women to shut the dog up. One of the women bent down, but the dog escaped her grasp and launched at Annie's leg. She kicked it off. The dog came back for more. Sam used the distraction to her advantage and left her position. Taser in hand, she ran into the house, charging ahead of Liam and Oliver who were in the hallway. They gave her the thumbs-up, and Sam thrust open the lounge door, hard enough for it to bounce back off the wall.

"Don't move, Annie. Drop the knife or I'll shoot."

"Fuck off, you wouldn't dare."

The images of the four charred victims flashed through Sam's mind, and she didn't hesitate. The woman dropped to the floor. Sam pleaded for the two female guests to call their dog back in case it attacked Annie and also received a shock. "Cuff her and get her out of my sight, boys."

Liam and Oliver stepped around Sam who had released her finger from the trigger. The rest of the team swept into the room which made it tight for space.

"Would someone mind telling us what's going on here?" the blonde guest asked, seemingly terrified by what she'd just witnessed.

"Let's get her out of here, and I'll explain the situation. You're safe, that's all that matters."

"Thank God. Why? Why come here brandishing a knife?"

"I'll fill you in once she's out of the way," Sam assured the two guests.

"You keep saying *she*. Who is this person?" the blonde asked.

Sam stepped forward, and despite Annie twisting her head from side to side, Sam removed the balaclava.

The two visitors stared at each other, dumbstruck, until the blonde spoke. "I don't understand, you were here earlier. I've been in touch with you for weeks, organising this trip. Why are you here?"

"Yes, go on, Annie, we'd all love to know the answer to that particular question," Sam prompted.

Annie took her time, glared at every single person in the room, and then shrugged. "Because you had to be punished."

"For what?" Sam demanded. "Why punish the couples who used the agency?"

"They have no right coming here. Driving on our roads, like maniacs most of the time. If it wasn't for them… he'd still be alive today."

"I swear we haven't done anything to this woman, we haven't got the foggiest idea what the heck she is talking about. This is the first time we've visited the area. Is she nuts? A crazy local or what?" the blonde asked.

"We know all about your husband, Annie. It was a tragic accident and yet you felt the need to punish innocent people, all young, just like Jake, killing them for one reason, because they chose to holiday in this area."

Annie tipped her head back and let out a sinister cackle. "And I would have succeeded for several months to come if you hadn't been on the case."

"I doubt it. You're not as smart as you think you are. Forensics would have found something on you sooner or later. Instead, this investigation was solved by good old-fashioned detective work. A major slip-up on your part, and it got the ball rolling."

"What was that?" Annie shouted, incensed.

Sam winked at her and nodded at Liam to take her away. "That's for me to know. You criminals need to learn you have to get out of bed early to catch me out."

EPILOGUE

Sam booked Annie Mitton in with the custody sergeant and informed her that she would be interviewed first thing in the morning.

Annie told her not to bother because she would go down the infuriating 'no comment' route.

Sam turned her back on the criminal and headed home for the evening, feeling she had accomplished something positive for the first time since before Chris had taken his own life.

Damn, I forgot the funeral is in the morning. Miss Mitton will have to stew in her cell a little while longer, unless I can twist Bob's arm into interviewing her.

THE FOLLOWING DAY DAWNED, and the day she had been dreading and planning for what seemed like a couple of weeks now, had arrived. She gave Sonny a huge cuddle and stretched out beside him for a few extra minutes before she began her day in earnest.

At eight forty-five, she called Bob, told him he would need to interview Annie first thing.

"Damn, I forgot the funeral was today. Don't you want me to be there?"

"There's no need for that, we both know it would be hypocritical of you to attend. You hated him as much as he hated you."

"Yeah, but I'd be supporting you, you need it, today of all days."

"I've got plenty of support, don't worry. My mum, dad, Crystal and Vernon will all be there."

"What about Chris's parents?"

"That's the part I'm not looking forward to. I had to contact his mother at the start, when I was working out all the arrangements. She was desperate to be involved. All was good in the beginning, but then she became overbearing with her needs, and I was forced to tell her to back off."

"Shit! I had no idea you were going through all that crap on your own, you should have told me."

"It's not in me to share every single detail of my life, Bob. I've coped, just about. Hey, you can help me out by getting Annie Mitton's confession nailed down this morning. Take Suzanna with you. I think it'll help having another female in the room with you."

"Good thinking. I'll do that. I'll ring you later, let you know how we got on. What time will you be heading out?"

"The funeral is due to start at eleven. I'll leave here at around ten-thirty with my family."

"Good luck. I mean this, Sam, you'll be in my thoughts and my heart today. Someone of your age should never have to go through something as traumatic as this. You're one hell of a woman, Sam Cobbs."

Her eyes sprung a leak at his unexpected commendation. "Get away with you. Thanks, partner, that means a lot to me.

I guess we both have a vitally important day ahead of us, in one form or another. Speak later, once it's all over."

"Take care, Sam."

THE DOORBELL RANG AT TEN. Her mother and father had arrived, bang on time as usual. She hugged her parents and apologised for sending her mother packing a few days earlier.

Her mother had the grace to forgive her with one of her loving smiles and another firm hug. "I know you wanted to do everything yourself, but there comes a time when you have to accept others' willingness to ease the burden now and again, Sam."

"One day I'll appreciate that fact, Mum. I just wanted to do the right thing for Chris, if only to give me a clear conscience."

"It's over with now," her father stated. "At least, it will be soon. Are we to expect fireworks from Chris's side of the family?"

Sam sighed and shrugged. "Who knows? His mother fell out with me a long time ago. I had minimal amount of contact with her after his death, but I made it clear that I wanted to give him a good sendoff. Let's just say things got tense pretty darn quickly. Who knows how she's going to react today, surrounded by her side of the family to give her courage?"

"She wouldn't dare, would she?" her mother asked.

"The truthful answer is, I don't know. Still, we'll find out soon enough."

The front door opened, and Crystal and Vernon walked in.

She hugged them both and smiled. "Thanks for being with me today."

"We wouldn't have it any other way," Crystal replied. "Umm… we passed the funeral car at the end of the road."

Sam's stomach flipped. "I suppose this is it then. Are we all ready? I just need to nip Sonny next door to Doreen."

"I'll do that," Vernon volunteered. "I'd like to meet the woman who is joint hound-sitter."

Sam nodded. "She'd love that. Send her my regards. Tell her I'll collect Sonny in a few hours, all being well."

She watched Sonny trot out of the room happily wagging his tail with Vernon by his side and sighed. "What did I ever do to deserve you all?"

"Hey, we're the lucky ones. Did I see on the news last night you solved another murder inquiry this week?" her father asked.

Sam's cheeks flushed. "I did. Or should I say, my team and I did, along with another couple of inspectors from other forces."

"You're remarkable. You had all of this to contend with as well. You never cease to amaze us, Sam," her father said.

"All in a day's work as they say."

The doorbell rang, interrupting their conversation before Sam had the chance to ruin her makeup with fresh tears. She answered the door to find the funeral director, Mr Woods, standing there.

"We're all set to go when you are. We'll take it nice and easy to the church, so we'll need to start off soon. Providing you're ready, of course."

"Thank you. Yes, we're all good to go." Sam peered at the black clouds darkening the sky overhead. "Let's hope the rain stays away."

"Weather forecast predicts it will arrive within the hour, so be prepared for that."

"It figures. Every funeral I've ever attended has been conducted in the rain."

"Part and parcel of our job, I'm afraid."

"I'll gather the troops and be with you in five minutes." Sam closed the door and exhaled a large breath to calm her heart rate.

The family set off as soon as Vernon returned. Sam waved and blew a kiss at Doreen from the garden gate. Her neighbour waved back and then wiped her eyes on the tissue she was holding.

AT THE CHURCH, Sam's sister clung to her arm throughout the service and also outside at the graveside. It wasn't until Chris's body had been placed in the grave that his mother approached Sam.

"Hello, Nancy. I hope I did you and your family proud today."

Nancy replied with a slap that sent Sam's head twisting to the right.

Stunned, she held a hand against her cheek.

"Now wait just a minute, that was uncalled for," Crystal scolded, coming to Sam's defence.

"Was it? If she hadn't kicked my son out of the house and their marriage, he'd still be alive today."

Sam held her head high and shoved back her shoulders. It was time the woman knew the truth about her angelic son. "Maybe if Chris had kept his penis in his pants, I wouldn't have asked for the divorce in the first place. He walked out on me. For three whole weeks, I didn't know where he was. You remember me ringing you, don't you?"

"I do."

"I found out, or should I say my partner spotted him one day, coming out of a woman's house. It turns out that he had been having an affair with her for months. So don't try and put the onus on me."

"We all make mistakes. He admitted he was wrong and tried to make amends, to get back with you, but what had you done…? Bloody moved on. You didn't hang around either, did you?"

"Now wait just a minute…" Crystal took a step towards Nancy.

Sam latched on to her arm, bringing her back. "Don't, Crystal. She's not worth it. I have nothing to feel guilty about. Even though Chris did the dirty and left me with a mountain of debts…"

Nancy gasped, yet another snippet her son had failed to tell her.

"… I still did right by him in the end, giving him a good sendoff."

"I had no idea," Nancy murmured.

"Why would you? He deceived us all in one way or another. I will never forgive him for doing what he did in front of me. I will have to live with the guilt of seeing him go up in flames like that. So don't ever try to make me feel bad about our failed marriage. He brought all this upon himself. When he started the fire, my whole future went up in flames with him. His final selfish act. Something for you to be proud of."

Chris's father shook his head. "There's no need for you to be so bitter, Sam. You'll never see or hear from us again. Come on, Nancy, let's go." He turned his wife by her shoulders and walked her away.

Crystal pulled Sam into her arms, and she blubbed like a baby. She opened her eyes to see Rhys standing behind her sister at the edge of the crowd.

He shuffled his feet, nervously, and then walked tentatively towards her. Sam withdrew from Crystal's arms and searched for a tissue in her pocket. Crystal followed Sam's gaze and stood aside.

"You came," Sam whispered.

Rhys held out his arms. "I couldn't let you do this by yourself. I'm sorry, Sam. Please forgive me, I was wrong to take Benji's death out on you."

Sam hushed him with a kiss. Her broken heart healed within seconds of having him close to her again.

Maybe life was for living after all. It would be foolish of her not to give it a final shot with Rhys, the man who had captured her heart.

THE END

THANK you for reading To Entice Them the next thrilling adventure To Control Them is now available.

HAVE you read any of my fast paced other crime thrillers yet? Why not try the first book in the DI Sara Ramsey series No Right to Kill

OR GRAB the first book in the bestselling, award-winning, Justice series here, Cruel Justice.

OR THE FIRST book in the spin-off Justice Again series, Gone In Seconds.

. . .

Perhaps you'd prefer to try one of my other police procedural series, the DI Kayli Bright series which begins with The Missing Children.

Or maybe you'd enjoy the DI Sally Parker series set in Norfolk, Wrong Place.

Or my gritty police procedural starring DI Nelson set in Manchester, Torn Apart.

Or maybe you'd like to try one of my successful psychological thrillers She's Gone, I KNOW THE TRUTH or Shattered Lives.

KEEP IN TOUCH WITH M A COMLEY

Pick up a FREE novella by signing up to my newsletter today.
https://BookHip.com/WBRTGW

BookBub
www.bookbub.com/authors/m-a-comley

Blog

http://melcomley.blogspot.com

Why not join my special Facebook group to take part in monthly giveaways.

Readers' Group